Dominic slowly closed the door behind him

"Sara," he groaned, pulling her into his arms, "I've been wanting this since—" His lips closed firmly on hers.

There was no thought of denial. Her mouth opened to accept the probing intimacy of his; her body arched against him. She had never been kissed so intimately, so thoroughly. Each touch of Dominic's lips was more drugging than the last.

The situation was spiraling out of control—Dominic's hands following the curve of her back sending shivers of delight down her spine, his mouth now caressing the hollow below her ear.

But she was a substitute—Marie's double. It wasn't her he was kissing at all. This realization made her spin away from him.

"I have to go," she said jerkily. "I—I'll wait for my father outside."

CAROLE MORTIMER
is also the author of these

Harlequin Presents

Many of these titles are available at your local bookseller.

For a free catalog listing all titles currently available,
send your name and address to:

HARLEQUIN READER SERVICE
1440 South Priest Drive, Tempe, AZ 85281
Canadian address: Stratford, Ontario N5A 6W2

CAROLE MORTIMER

forbidden surrender

Harlequin Books

TORONTO • NEW YORK • LOS ANGELES • LONDON
AMSTERDAM • PARIS • SYDNEY • HAMBURG
STOCKHOLM • ATHENS • TOKYO • MILAN

For
John and Matthew

—————◆—————

Harlequin Presents first edition November 1982
ISBN 0-373-10547-9

Original hardcover edition published in 1982
by Mills & Boon Limited

CHAPTER ONE

'MARIE! How are you?'

Sara blinked up at the tall attractive man in front of her, smiling her regret. 'I'm sorry,' her American accent was very noticeable against his English one, 'I'm afraid you have the wrong person.' She turned away with an apologetic smile, wishing that she could have been the absent Marie. This man was very good-looking, possibly in his mid-twenties, and by the expression in his twinkling blue eyes he looked as if he could be fun to be around.

He took hold of her arm, stopping her from crossing the road. 'Hey, I'm not going to tell Nick that you were wandering around Soho on your own.'

Sara frowned, her deep brown eyes puzzled, a startling contrast to her long golden-blonde hair, hair bleached by years under the Florida sun. Having lived in America most of her life she had been curious to see the country she had been born in, the country she had lived in until she was a year old, taken to start a new life in America by her mother after the untimely death of her husband.

'I'm sorry,' she repeated to the young man, 'but you really are mistaken.'

He remained unconvinced. 'I love the accent,' he grinned, 'but I know you too well to be fooled by that.' He put his arm about her waist, his fingers spread dangerously close to her breast.

Sara stiffened, revising her opinion of him. He was obviously a flirt, and he sounded as if he and Marie were more than just casual acquaintances.

She gave him a cold stare. 'Would you kindly take your hands off me?' she requested haughtily, flicking

7

her long hair back over her shoulder.

He frowned down at her but made no effort to let her go. 'There's no need to be like this, Marie. I admit I'm a bit sore about the way you ended things between us last year, but Nick——'

Sara squirmed away from him. 'I don't know any Nick, and I don't know you either. And if you don't let go of me I'll call a policeman!' She looked around for one, never having thought a man would try to pick her up so openly. It was the middle of the afternoon, she had got lost during a sightseeing session, and she certainly hadn't expected to be accosted like this.

'Okay, okay,' the man grimaced, 'there's no need to get nasty. If you want to keep up this pretence of being an American tourist then that's all right with me.' He shrugged.

She wasn't pretending to be anything, an American tourist was exactly what she was, although this wasn't a very high class area to have got lost in. She only hoped Aunt Susan didn't go home without her. Only having been in this country a couple of days herself she had no idea of the way back to Aunt Susan's house.

'Maybe I could be your guide?' The man gave her a sideways glance. 'Hey, that could be fun, Marie. We could——'

'I already have a guide,' she interrupted him, annoyed by the fact that he still believed her to be this other woman. It would seem he knew Marie very well, which made his obstinacy about her identity all the more surprising. Unless this was the way he usually picked his women up!

'Oh, I see,' he smiled bitterly. 'I bet Nick doesn't know about this—and I wish to God I didn't!' He bent and kissed her briefly on the mouth. 'See you at the weekend,' was his parting shot.

Sara stared after him dazedly. She wasn't a prude, she had been kissed before, but never by a complete stranger. And he had been so respectable to look at too, his black pinstriped suit and snowy white shirt immaculate.

'Sara!' Her plump Aunt Susan arrived breathlessly in front of her. 'Thank goodness I've found you!'

Sara turned, the flirtatious stranger already swallowed up in the crowd. 'I must have lost you in that last shop,' she smiled her apology.

Susan Ford was a pleasantly plump lady of forty-eight, her blonde hair kept the same gold as Sara's by a light tint every couple of months, her face still youthfully smooth and attractive. She was Sara's mother's sister, and although the sisters had been parted for the last twenty years their letters to each other had been numerous, so much so that Sara felt as if she already knew her aunt when they had met two days ago, had found herself instantly liking her aunt.

This trip to England wasn't exactly a holiday to Sara, more of a convalescence. Six months ago her mother and stepfather had been killed in a car accident, and besides leaving her orphaned it had also left her with two broken legs, utterly ruining the modelling career that had just been starting to take off the ground.

It had taken six months for the scars to heal, both the emotional and physical ones, and on her final dismissal from the doctor she had arranged this trip to visit her English relatives, finding herself to be a very rich young woman on the death of her stepfather, Richard Hamille. They had been a close family, Sara being adopted by Richard when he had married her mother, and to suddenly find herself alone was very bewildering.

Her Aunt Susan had instantly taken her to her heart, she and Uncle Arthur having no children of their own. Sara felt at home with them, felt at home with England, and in a way she would be sad to leave when the time came. Still, that wouldn't be for another couple of weeks yet.

'Who was that man?' her aunt frowned. 'The one I saw you talking to?'

Sara shrugged as they fell into step together, making their way back to the busy city centre. 'I have no idea,' she answered her aunt.

Her eyes widened. 'You didn't know him?'

Sara shook her head. 'No.'

'But I saw him kiss you!' Her aunt sounded scandalised.

Sara grinned. 'I think he was trying to pick me up. It wasn't a very good approach, though—he pretended that he thought I was someone else.' She shook her head. 'Not very original!'

'Who did he think you were?'

She shrugged. 'Someone called Marie. I wouldn't have minded, but he seemed so insistent. Oh well,' she dismissed, 'he'll have to chalk this one down to a no-go.'

'Yes, I suppose so,' her aunt agreed vaguely. 'Now, where were we? Oh yes, if we turn here we should be near the underground. Shall we go home and have a cup of tea? I'm dying for a cup.'

Sara grinned at her, her face alight with mischief, her features strikingly beautiful, the eyes wide and a deep dark brown, heavily fringed by long black lashes, the nose short, the mouth wide and smiling, her teeth very white against her golden skin. Her body was tall and supple, long-legged, and very slender. Her looks were invaluable in her profession, and she hoped to return to modelling when she went back to the States.

'You and your tea!' she chided. After only two days she was well aware of her aunt's weakness for the brew, the other woman seeming to drink gallons of the stuff. Sara preferred coffee herself, but she readily agreed with the idea of going home for refreshment; the visit to Buckingham Palace and the Houses of Parliament had tired her out.

Uncle Arthur came in soon after they did, a short

stocky man, going a little thin on top, his sparse brown hair going slightly grey now.

'I have a surprise for you, love,' he beamed at Sara as they ate their dinner. 'I've invited Eddie round tonight, my nephew by my sister Jean. I thought you would like a bit of young company for a change.'

Sara masked her irritation. Her aunt and uncle had been so kind to her, and it was ungrateful of her not to appreciate this extra act of kindness. They had no way of knowing of her recent disillusionment, of the way Barry had let her down when she needed him the most, had walked out on her when the accident had temporarily robbed her of the ability to walk into a room with him and make one of his grand entrances. Barry was an up-and-coming actor, had appeared in several television serials, and he ranked his worth much higher than any television producer had yet had the foresight to do. Sara had been dating him a couple of months before the accident, not realising that her main attraction had been her undeniable beauty and her original way of dressing. Barry had replaced her within a day of the accident, having no time for her bereavement or her own injuries.

So at the moment she wasn't particularly keen on men. 'That will be nice,' she gave a bright smile.

'I hope so,' her uncle nodded, settling back in his armchair. 'He's a good lad, works in a garage.'

'He doesn't work in a garage, Arthur,' his wife chided. 'He owns one, dear,' she told Sara. 'And he lets other people do the work.'

Sara felt sure Eddie wouldn't agree with that, the poor man was probably worked off his feet. It wasn't easy running a business, she knew that. Her stepfather had run an advertising firm, and he had often come home absolutely exhausted. Eddie probably felt the same way on occasion.

'It's nice of him to spare me the time,' she said in all honesty.

'Well, he took a bit of persuading,' her uncle told her, 'but I managed to talk him round.'

After Barry's desertion of her this wasn't exactly a booster to her morale. It was because of Eddie's apparent reluctance to meet her that she took special care over her appearance that evening.

Her silky suit was in a pale lilac colour, the narrow belt that fitted over the shirt top in a deep purple colour. Her shoes matched the colour of the belt, her legs were long and silky beneath the straight skirt. She was aiming to knock his eyes out, so her make-up was dramatic, just to show him that his time hadn't been wasted.

When she heard him arrive she checked her appearance. Her hair, newly washed, fell in gentle waves halfway down her back, shaped in casual curls either side of her face. Yes, she looked the top model she had rapidly been becoming until the accident, and if Eddie wasn't impressed now he never would be.

He was. It was obvious by the widening of his deep blue eyes, by the way he slowly rose to his feet, his gaze appraising.

'Hi,' she greeted huskily, giving him her most dazzling smile. 'I'm Sara, and you must be Eddie.' She held out her hand politely.

He took her hand, seemingly reluctant to let it go again. His own hand was strong and work-worn, the nails kept short and clean. He was a man possibly in his late twenties, his hair sandy-blond, his face attractive, his dress casual in the extreme, his denims faded, his shirt unbuttoned partway down his chest.

'Nice to meet you,' he gave a wide appreciative smile. 'Uncle Arthur didn't tell me how—Well, he didn't say— You're gorgeous!' he grinned.

Sara gave a happy laugh, at last managing to release her hand. 'Thank you, kind sir,' she curtseyed. 'Uncle Arthur wasn't too descriptive about you either,' she admitted, instantly liking this man.

Eddie nodded understandingly. 'You expected me to

be wearing an overall, with oil under my fingernails,' he derided.

'Something like that,' she gave a rueful smile. 'Although Aunt Susan assured me you didn't actually work in your garage.' Her eyes twinkled mischievously.

'Charming!'

She burst out laughing at his disgusted expression. 'I'm sure she didn't mean it the way I made it sound.' Her aunt and uncle had taken advantage of Eddie's visit and gone to visit some friends for the evening.

'Hey, you're all right,' Eddie smiled at her. 'Fancy coming out for a pint? A beer,' he explained at her puzzled expression.

'I'd love to,' she accepted eagerly.

She had never been into a 'local' before, had never even been into a bar. Her mother and stepfather were quite protective of her, vetting most of her friends, and keeping her close within their own circle.

She loved the pub they went to, loved the beer Eddie made her try, loved the friendly, warm atmosphere, and most of all she loved the people. She was instantly accepted into Eddie's crowd and persuaded to join in a game of darts, a game she was totally hopeless at. But she had a lot of fun trying, and no one seemed to mind her inability to hit the board twice in a row.

'That was fun!' She gave Eddie a glowing smile on the drive back to her aunt and uncle's house.

'Glad you enjoyed it. Care to come out with me again?' He quirked one eyebrow enquiringly.

'I'd love to!' Sara's face glowed.

'Tomorrow?'

She looked uncertain. 'I'm not sure what plans Aunt Susan and Uncle Arthur have for me. You see——'

'It's okay, Sara,' he cut in dryly, 'I realise I'm not the sort of man you usually go out with.'

She blushed at his intended rebuke. 'I didn't mean that.'

'But it's true, isn't it? You were like a child tonight, enjoyed each new experience with eagerness. Uncle Arthur told me you were a rich kid, in the executive bracket.'

Sara bit her lip, knowing she had hurt him. 'I did enjoy tonight, and I—I'm sorry if I embarrassed you with my enthusiasm. I didn't mean to.'

Eddie sighed. 'You didn't. You were a success, you know you were. Maybe that's why I'm so annoyed—I was jealous of half the men there tonight.'

Sara relaxed somewhat, back on territory she could handle. 'You had no need to be. I always remember who took me on my date, and I always make a point of leaving with that person.'

'So it's still on for tomorrow, if Aunt Susan and Uncle Arthur don't have any other plans for you? And this time I'll take you somewhere I can have you all to myself.'

She wasn't so sure his single-minded interest was a good thing. She would be going back to the States soon, two or three weeks at the most, and it wouldn't do for Eddie to become involved with her, not deeply involved. When she got back home she intended concentrating exclusively on her career, there would be no time for romantic involvement.

'Sara?' Eddie prompted.

'I—er—What did you have in mind?'

He shrugged. 'A meal and then on to a club?'

'It sounds lovely,' she accepted, deciding she could deal with Eddie's interest in her if and when it started to become serious. She liked him, he was fun, and there could be no harm in them going out together. 'What time shall I be ready?'

'Oh, about eight.' He stopped the car outside the house.

'Like to come in for coffee?' she invited.

'Not tonight, thanks. If I know Aunt Susan and Uncle Arthur they'll have gone to bed long ago, and I wouldn't want to disturb them. You'd better ask them for a door key for tomorrow, we could be late.'

'Not too late, I hope,' Sara frowned. 'I need my beauty sleep,' she added lightly.

'I hadn't noticed,' he teased.

She smiled. 'I really don't want to be too late. I—I don't keep late hours any more.' Since leaving the hospital she had taken life at a slow pace, retiring early and rising late.

'Okay,' Eddie sighed. 'I'll have you home by midnight—Cinderella. But I should still ask for a key, they're usually in bed by ten.'

She knew that, and for the last two nights she had done the same thing. 'I'll ask,' she promised. 'And thanks once again for tonight, I had a great time.'

'Enough of a great time to kiss me goodnight?'

She leant forward and kissed him lightly on the mouth. 'Goodnight,' she called before hurrying into the house.

They had both been wrong; their aunt and uncle weren't in bed at all, they were still in the lounge.

'But it's still worrying,' Aunt Susan could be heard insisting.

'You're worrying over nothing,' her husband chided her. 'Just forget about it, it didn't mean a thing.'

'But, Arthur——'

'Susan!' he said sternly. 'I think I just heard Sara come in, so let's just drop the subject.'

Sara shrugged to herself, coughing to let them know of her presence. Her mother and stepfather often had minor arguments, but they usually passed within a day or so, and she felt sure things were no different between her aunt and uncle, the middle-aged couple seemed very happy together.

'Did you have a nice time, dear?' her aunt asked as she came into the room.

'Lovely,' she nodded agreement.

'Going out with him again?' Uncle Arthur eyed her

over the top of his horn-rimmed glasses.

Sara blushed. 'Tomorrow.'

'Hear that, Susan?' he turned to his wife. 'Before you know it we'll have a wedding on our hands.'

'Arthur!' she warned.

'I'm not getting married for years yet, Uncle Arthur,' Sara told him hastily. 'I'm only twenty, almost twenty-one.'

'Susan and I had already been married two years by that time.'

'It was different when we were young, Arthur,' his wife chided. 'There's so much for young people to do nowadays, places to see, that they don't want to tie themselves down to marriage too young.'

He raised his eyebrows, his eyes twinkling with mischief. 'After all these years she finally tells me she married me out of boredom!' He winked at Sara.

'Go on with you!' his wife scorned. 'Where's Eddie taking you tomorrow?' she turned to ask Sara.

'Out to dinner and then on to a club, he said.' Her aunt and uncle's interest in her evening out was nothing unusual to Sara, her mother had always been interested in such things too, and it was in fact quite like home sitting and chatting like this after an enjoyable evening out.

'Better than a trip to a pub,' Uncle Arthur teased.

'I liked the pub.' Sara had been quite disappointed that Eddie had decided not to take her back there.

Aunt Susan stood up, putting down her knitting. 'Well, I'm for bed. Arthur?'

'I am too.' He stood up, stretching. 'It's nice having you with us, love,' he told Sara huskily.

She moved to hug him, tears in her eyes. 'It's nice to be here. I wish now I'd come sooner, instead of waiting until——' she broke off, stricken.

Her uncle patted her shoulder awkwardly. 'It's all right, Sara. We're your family now, for as long as you want us.'

'Thank you.' She kissed them both on the cheek before hurrying to her room.

The tears flowed readily once she closed her bedroom door; the loss of her parents was still a raw wound. Without Aunt Susan and Uncle Arthur's support the last few days she didn't know what she would have done; some of the moods of depression she had suffered in the States had been very black indeed.

After an exhaustive perusal of most of the museums the next day Sara didn't feel up to going anywhere that evening. But she had told Eddie she would go out with him and she couldn't let him down. If they were dining out he had probably had to book a table.

'Oh, you look lovely!' her aunt exclaimed as Sara came into the lounge to wait for Eddie.

She felt quite confident of her appearance, knowing her black dress would be suitable for any occasion, would blend in both at the restaurant and the club, its style demure while still managing to show the perfection of her figure, her breasts firm and uptilting, the slenderness of her waist emphasised by a thick black belt, her hips narrow in the pencil-slim styling of the dress. Her legs were long and smooth, her slender ankles shown to advantage in the high-heeled sandals she wore, a slender gold chain about one of her ankles. She had needed to wear it for one of her photographic sessions, and now found it an attractive piece of jewellery.

She sat down opposite her aunt, her long hair secured on the top of her head, leaving her neck slenderly vulnerable. 'Where's Uncle Arthur?'

'Gone for a drink with a few of his friends.' Her aunt carried on with her knitting, halfway through making a cardigan for her husband. 'It's a regular thing. It does him good to get out for an evening.'

Sara frowned. 'You should have told me, then I wouldn't have arranged to go out tonight.'

'You go out and have a good time,' she encouraged. 'To tell you the truth,' she confided with a smile. 'I usually doze off about nine o'clock.'

'I see,' Sara laughed. 'A bit of peace and quiet, hmm?'

'That's the idea. That will be Eddie,' Aunt Susan said as the doorbell rang.

Sara went and answered the door herself. Eddie was looking very smart in a navy blue suit and contrasting light blue shirt. His eyes widened as he saw her. 'You're ready.' He stepped into the hallway.

'Of course,' she frowned. 'It's eight o'clock, isn't it?'

'Oh yes,' he nodded. 'I just thought I'd be kept waiting until at least eight-fifteen.'

She smiled as she led the way back to the lounge. 'I always try to be punctual. My mother always told me that if someone has taken the trouble to arrive on time then it's only polite to be ready.'

Eddie smiled. 'I think I would have liked your mother.'

They said their goodbyes to Aunt Susan. The drive to the restaurant was a short one, their table secluded in one of the corners of the room.

'I quite like Chinese food myself,' Eddie told her once they had given their order. 'But not knowing your preferences I played it safe and chose an English restaurant.'

Sara eyed him teasingly. 'You were taking a risk thinking I like to eat at all. Most of the models I know live on milk and lettuce leaves.'

'Hey, that's right—you're a model, aren't you? Are you open to offers? And I meant for work,' he added dryly.

She shrugged. 'I will be, when I get back to the States. I don't have a permit to work over here. This trip is strictly pleasure.'

'Pity. I have a friend who's a photographer. No, really,' he insisted at her dubious expression. 'Pete and I were at school together. He's quite successful over here.'

'Maybe some other time,' Sara said regretfully.

'Okay. Maybe I'll be able to introduce the two of you before you go home, then you'll have a contact over here if you ever should decide to work here.'

Sara smiled, her skin a glowing peach colour, her eyes deeply brown. 'That's really nice of you, thank you.'

'No trouble,' Eddie dismissed.

It was after ten when they left the restaurant for the club, by now the two of them firm friends. Sara's eyes were glowing from the amount of wine she had consumed during her meal, her smile more ready than usual.

The club was plush and exclusive, not really the sort of place she would have thought Eddie would have enjoyed frequenting.

'I know what you're thinking,' Eddie grimaced. 'But I've been here a couple of times with Pete.' He shrugged. 'I like watching the rich lose their money.' He referred to the gambling tables, jewel-bedecked women and quietly affluent men gazing avidly down at the tables. 'Pete's a member,' he explained the fact that they had actually been able to get in. 'And the people here know me.'

Sara felt slightly uncomfortable among such people. 'That sounds as if you've been here more than a couple of times,' she teased.

He looked sheepish. 'Maybe a few.'

She put her arm through his, determinedly putting any feelings of shyness behind her. 'Let's go and take a look.'

She had never been in a gambling club before, and for the first half hour she found it all fascinating. They were standing behind a middle-aged woman, who to Sara's knowledge systematically lost every bet she placed. Sara stood back away from the light, finding it all very sickening, was the only word she could think of to describe that mindless addiction.

'I'll get you a drink,' Eddie suggested.

She would rather have left, but she didn't want to be a killjoy. Eddie was enjoying himself, and they would probably be leaving quite soon. She accepted the offer of a drink, continuing to watch the play in front of her, not understanding it at all but becoming more and more fascinated by the spin of the roulette wheel as she waited for Eddie's return.

A woman on the other side of the table finally gave up, standing up to leave. A man moved to take her place, and Sara watched him as he began to win. This man had the look of an experienced gambler, a deadpan face, his blue eyes shrewd.

Sara watched him, her interest in the roulette re-awakened. His movements were made without haste, his hands slender and lean, the fingers long and tapered. Her eyes were drawn from his hands to his face—a hard face, the deep blue eyes narrowed, the nose hawk-like, the mouth compressed, his jaw set at a strong angle. The evening suit he wore was impeccably styled, as was his dark over-long hair, his manner assured and speaking of wealth. The staff of the club treated him with deep respect, making Sara wonder who he could be. He was in his mid-thirties, maybe a little younger, and yet he seemed to be a man of affluence.

Suddenly he looked up and caught her watching him, and his face darkened into a frown, any attractiveness about him instantly disappearing. She recoiled from the angry dislike in his blazing blue eyes and turned away in search of Eddie. He was a long time getting their drinks.

Someone grasped her arm and she was roughly spun around to face the man she had been watching at the roulette table. He must have left the table immediately she turned away.

'What the hell are you doing here?' he rasped, his fingers painful on her arm.

Sara frowned at this attack on her, both physically

and verbally. 'I—We—I was signed in.'

His mouth twisted—a perfect mouth, the lower lip fuller, pointing to a sensuality this man would take pains to hide. 'So you aren't alone?'

'No——'

The man pulled her away from the table and over to a quiet corner of the room—if it could be called quiet in a room like this. 'Who are you with?' he demanded to know.

'I—Let me go!' Sara tried to pry his fingers loose, looking up at him with wide apprehensive eyes. If she had done something wrong by being here why didn't he just say so and let her leave? There was no need for him to get rough with her. And where was Eddie? He could explain that he had signed her in, that his friend was a member. 'You're hurting me!' she cried as his strong fingers refused to be dislodged from her arm.

His teeth snapped together, white teeth, very even. 'I'd like to do more than that!' He thrust her away from him. 'Who's the man?' he asked tautly.

Sara rubbed her bruised skin. 'Eddie Mayer,' she muttered.

The man's expression was grim, frighteningly so. 'I don't know him, but then I never do, do I? Well, you got this Eddie Mayer to bring you, so he can damn well take you home again. We'll discuss this tomorrow.'

She blinked up at him. 'Tomorrow . . .?'

'Yes, tomorrow. And make sure you're there. I'm getting a little tired of these exploits of yours, Marie. I thought they were over,' he sighed. 'God, if your father knew . . .' He shook his head.

It was Marie again! For the second time in two days she had been mistaken for this other girl, Marie. This man must be another of her men, and the man Nick that the man of yesterday had warned her about was obviously this girl's father. Considering she didn't know the girl she was finding out a lot about her!

Well, this man was a definite improvement on yesterday's, although he was no less wrong about her identification. 'There's been a mistake——'

'Yes,' he hissed angrily, 'and I'm beginning to think I made it!' He gave her a disgusted look. 'We'll talk tomorrow.' He turned and walked out of the club with long controlled strides.

Sara was left feeling as if she had just survived an earthquake, or something equally disastrous. Whoever this Marie was she led an interesting and varied life, and it looked as if this last man had had enough. The other girl was obviously a flirt, but that didn't make it right that she was going to get the blame for something she hadn't done.

She was curious to know the man's identity, and walked over to the doorman. 'That man . . .' she paused hesitantly. 'The one that just left . . .'

'Mr Thorne?' the man enquired politely.

'Oh, Mr Thorne,' she feigned disappointment. 'It seems I made a mistake, I thought it was Gerrard Turner,' she hastily made a name up.

'No, miss,' the doorman shook his head, 'that was Mr Dominic Thorne. He's in engineering.'

'Thank you,' she smiled. 'Wrong man,' she shrugged before walking away.

When the man said Dominic Thorne was 'in engineering' she felt sure he meant that he ran these firms. There had been an air of authority about the man, a determination that wouldn't let him be ruled by anyone. Despite his rough treatment of her Sara had found him attractive. A shame he was interested in someone called Marie, a girl who appeared to be her double.

She had read that everyone had a double somewhere in the world, but it seemed hers was living in London, and that their likeness was so extreme that even this Marie's lovers seemed to have been fooled. And Sara was sure both those men had been her lovers; they had both had a strong sense of familiarity about them towards her—or rather, Marie.

'Sara!' Eddie appeared in front of her. 'I thought for a minute you'd left without me,' he sighed his relief. 'Sorry I was so long, but I ran into Pete. Come over and meet him.'

She went willingly enough, just relieved to have him back with her, before any more of Marie's men accosted her. Pete proved to be an extrovert, even the sober suit and tie did not diminish his exuberant nature.

'Wow!' he exclaimed when he saw her, pulling her on to the bar stool next to him. 'I bet you're a natural,' he enthused, studying her with the practised eye of a photographer. 'Boy, would I like to get you the other side of my camera,' he spoke softly to himself. 'No chance of that?' He quirked a hopeful eyebrow.

Sara grinned at him; this enthusiasm was doing wonders for her ego. 'Not this trip,' she refused him. 'I've already explained to Eddie that I don't have a permit——'

'I could get you one,' Pete cut in eagerly.

She shook her head. 'I'm still convalescing.'

'Mm, Eddie explained.' Pete was studying her closely. 'Have you ever worked in this country?'

'I've never even been here before, except as a baby, so I certainly haven't worked here before.'

'I have this feeling I've seen you before.' He frowned his puzzlement.

'Not you too!' Sara sighed. 'You're the third one since I've been here.'

'At the club?' Eddie enquired, sitting the other side of her.

'No, in England. People keep thinking I'm someone else.'

'A pick-up!' he dismissed.

'No,' she shook her head. 'The first time it happened I thought that, but it happened again tonight, here, and both men thought I was the same person.' She shrugged her puzzlement.

Eddie put his arm about her shoulders. 'I refuse to

believe there are two like you,' he smiled at her warmly. 'Nature couldn't have been that generous!'

Sara ignored the pointed show of possession, realising that Eddie was warning his friend off her. Not that she particularly minded, one man was complication enough for her stay here. 'It was all very odd, though. Still,' she dismissed it from her mind, 'it doesn't matter. Could we possibly leave now, Eddie? It's getting late, and Aunt Susan and Uncle Arthur seem to have taken to waiting up for me.'

They made their goodbyes to Pete, and Sara promised to get in touch with him if she ever decided to work in England.

'Lucky we ran into him,' Eddie remarked on the drive home. 'He can be an elusive man, impossible to find at times.'

Sara was preoccupied, unable to put the thought of the man at the casino out of her mind. He hadn't been the sort of individual you forgot in a hurry; his manner was forceful, his attractiveness mesmerising, animally sensual. Whoever Marie was she was a lucky girl to have had him for a lover.

'Eddie,' she bit her lip thoughtfully, 'tonight, at the club, there was a man called Dominic Thorne. Do you know him?'

He spluttered with laughter. 'You have to be joking! He's out of my league, love,' he added less scornfully.

'But you have heard of him?'

'Who hasn't?' he shrugged, halting the car outside the house. 'He has his finger in every business pie going, every one that's legal, that is. He and his partner—well, his father's partner, actually, but the old man's dead now—they're in the millionaire class.'

'Is he married?' Sara made the query as casually as she could, not wanting to show her extreme interest in Eddie's answer.

'No,' he grinned. 'But he's going to be. He's done the

sensible thing, he's got himself engaged to his partner's daughter, Marie Lindlay.'

Sara swallowed hard. 'Marie . . .?'

'Mm. One day Dominic Thorne will have it all, all the business interests plus the lovely Marie.'

Sara was no longer listening to him. This Marie everyone kept confusing her with was actually going to *marry* Dominic Thorne. Surely he couldn't mistake another woman for the girl he was going to marry?

CHAPTER TWO

IT was all a puzzle to Sara, one there seemed no answer to. She mentioned it to her aunt, but she dismissed it as a coincidence.

'But even her fiancé thought I was this other girl,' Sara frowned.

Her aunt shrugged. 'It was dark in there, it was probably just a case of mistaken identity.'

'It feels weird to be so like another person.'

'Maybe you aren't really,' Aunt Susan dismissed. 'As I said, the lighting probably wasn't very good in this club you went to. Mr Thorne's girl-friend probably has blonde hair too, and in a bad light maybe you do have a resemblance to this other girl. I should just forget about it, Sara.'

'I suppose so,' she sighed. 'Although it might be interesting to actually see this Marie Lindlay.'

'Is that her name?'

'Eddie says it is,' she nodded.

'I—Oh, damn!' Her aunt swore as she dropped a cup, watching in dismay as it smashed on the floor. 'One of my best set, too,' she tutted, bending down to pick up the pieces. 'I hope they're still making these, I'd like to buy a replacement for it.' She put the pieces in the bin.

'I'm sure they do.' Sara swept up the shattered fragments still scattered on the floor.

Her uncle came into the room. 'Did I hear a crash just now?'

'It's as well I hadn't fallen over,' his wife snapped. 'It took you long enough to get in here.'

He looked taken aback by this unexpected attack. 'I knew Sara was in here helping you wash up.' He frowned. 'It was only a crash, Susan, not a thump.'

'It's all right, Uncle Arthur,' Sara soothed. 'Aunt Susan's just broken one of her best china cups, and I'm afraid she's rather upset about it. Take her into the lounge and I'll make you both a nice cup of tea.'

He nodded. 'Come on, Susan. It was only a cup,' he chided as they went through to the lounge.

'It wasn't that, Arthur. It was——' The kitchen door closed, cutting off the rest of the conversation.

Poor Aunt Susan, the tea-set obviously meant a lot to her. It was rather lovely to look at, very delicately made, with an old-fashioned floral pattern. She would see if she could get a replacement this afternoon when she went shopping.

'Where's Eddie taking you tonight?' her uncle asked as she took their cups of tea into them.

'I'm not seeing him tonight.' She had turned down his invitation for this evening, deciding that three nights in a row was just too much. 'But he's taking me out for a drive tomorrow,' she added ruefully. Eddie had been adamant about seeing her again, and she had finally agreed to let him drive her to see some of the English countryside.

London was interesting, there was certainly plenty to see, but she was well aware that there was a lot more to England than its capital. Her mother had never forgotten the greenness of the countryside here, it had been the one thing she really missed by living in America, and Sara was determined to see some of it before she left.

'As long as it isn't another casino,' her aunt shook her head disapprovingly.

Sara laughed. 'It was quite an experience.'

'Not one I'd like to see repeated,' Aunt Susan said sternly. 'I gave him a piece of my mind last night after you'd gone to bed. Taking you to a gambling hall, indeed!' she added disgustedly.

'You make it sound like a den of iniquity,' her husband teased.

'I'm sure Rachel wouldn't have approved of Sara going to such a place, and I don't either. And Eddie introduced Sara to that mad friend Pete of his.'

Uncle Arthur smiled. 'He isn't mad, Susan. A bit of an extrovert maybe, but there's no harm in him.'

It wasn't like her aunt to be bad-tempered, and Sara could only assume that breaking the cup had upset her more than they had realised.

She managed to find a replacement that afternoon, although she seemed to have walked most of London to find it. Her aunt was suitably pleased with her purchase.

'Eddie telephoned while you were out.' Her aunt put the cup with the rest of the set.

Sara looked up. 'Did he happen to say what he wanted?'

Her aunt smiled. 'He didn't "happen" to say at all—I asked him. He said something about a party tonight.'

'I see,' she bit her lip. 'He'll be calling back, then?'

'Mm. Soon, I should think.'

Ten minutes later a call came through, only this time it was Pete. 'Do you fancy going to a party?' he asked her.

'I think Eddie intends inviting me to one,' she refused.

'On my behalf. I'm the one who wants to take you to the party, Eddie has to work.'

Sara bristled angrily. 'I went out with Eddie because he's my uncle's nephew, I don't expect to be passed around to Eddie's friends!'

'Hey,' Pete chided, 'that isn't the idea at all.'

'Then what is?' she snapped.

'I suddenly realised why I thought you'd worked in this country before, and I wondered if you would like to meet your double.'

'Double . . .?' she repeated dazedly.

'Mm, you look exactly like Marie Lindlay.'

Sara frowned. Again someone had noticed the similarity. Her curiosity was aroused once again. To be able to see this girl, to see exactly what their similarity was, would be fun, even if this apparent likeness turned out to be a myth in the end.

'What sort of party is it?' she delayed making a decision.

'Given to amuse the idle rich,' he scorned.

'Then how did you get an invitation?' she teased, her anger leaving her.

'Naughty!' Pete chided. 'Actually I'm a friend of a friend, and I have it on good authority that Marie Lindlay is going to be there, with her fiancé, no less.'

Dominic Thorne. It would be interesting to see his face when he saw her, and at least she would be able to prove to him that his fiancée was telling the truth when she denied being at the club the evening before. Besides, she just wanted to get another look at him, to see if he really was as good-looking as her imagination told her he was.

'Okay,' she agreed. 'What shall I wear?' She didn't want to turn up wearing completely the wrong outfit.

'As little as possible.' She could almost hear Pete grinning. 'To tell you the truth, I usually take one of my models to these parties, and she wears the most shocking clothes. I like to make an entrance,' he added with homour.

Another one! 'Right.' Sara knew exactly the dress she was going to wear. 'I'll be ready at eight.'

'Make it nine,' Pete advised. 'These parties rarely get going until at least ten-thirty.'

'And the later we are the more of an entrance we can make,' Sara guessed dryly, knowing this from her experiences with Barry. 'Okay, nine it is.'

She was searching through her clothes in her wardrobe when her aunt came into the room. She had just found the gold dress and matching cape, and she quickly buried them beneath her other clothing. Aunt Susan would certainly not approve.

'Dinner's ready,' her aunt told her.

'So am I,' Sara smiled. 'I'm starving!'

She mentioned the party as they were eating their meal, and her uncle talked down Aunt Susan's objections.

'Let the girl enjoy herself,' he said affectionately. 'Lord knows she'll be leaving us soon enough.'

'But, Arthur——'

'Stop fussing, woman!' Sara's usually mild uncle spoke very firmly. 'Sara's quite old enough to know what she's doing. Pete may seem a little on the wild side to us, but to Sara I'm sure he seems a lot of fun.'

'He does,' she grinned, agreeing with her uncle. There was no harm in Pete, he was just a joker.

'Then that's all that matters. Are there any more potatoes, Susan?' He quirked an eyebrow at his wife.

She gave an impatient sigh. 'I thought you were starting your diet today?'

He grinned. 'It can wait until tomorrow.'

His wife gave a reluctant smile. 'I thought you might say that, which is why I did the normal amount of potatoes.' She went into the kitchen to get them.

Sara's uncle turned to wink at her. 'After thirty years she knows me better than I know myself.'

Sara hoped, if she ever got married, that she and her husband were as happy together after being married the same number of years.

She was glad of the cape top when she was at last dressed in the gold dress, it served to hide the scantiness of the gown's bodice. The material barely covered her naked breasts, completely strapless, the sheath of material clinging to every smooth curve of her body. With the cape about her shoulders, covering her naked shoulders and partially revealed breasts, the gown was still daring, but not as much as when the cape was removed.

When she heard Pete at the door she put her head around the lounge door and made her hurried goodbyes, dashing outside to join Pete before her aunt and uncle could see what she was wearing, not because she was ashamed of the dress but because she knew they wouldn't understand why she was wearing it. A dress like this would be perfectly acceptable in the company she would be mixing in this evening, in fact she had attended a party with her parents in it, but she was sure her aunt and uncle would be slightly shocked by its daring.

Pete wasn't so much shocked as delighted. 'Beautiful,' he murmured appreciatively.

Sara gave a happy laugh. 'Stop drooling and drive,' she ordered.

He did, driving to the more exclusive part of London. The cars in the driveway they finally arrived at were all in the expensive Rolls-Royce and Jaguar bracket. Pete's car was a Jaguar too, a vintage model, so it wasn't in the least out of place.

He grinned at her appreciation of it as he locked the doors. 'I bought it cheap. It was a wreck when I found it,' he explained. 'Eddie did it up for me.'

'Nice to have a friend who can see to your cars for you,' she teased.

'A friend who doesn't mind me taking his girl out for the evening,' he raised one eyebrow questioningly.

Her smile faded. 'I'm not his girl, Pete. We're just friends.'

'I know,' he grinned. 'Eddie told me he'd been politely but firmly warned off. Don't worry, Sara,' he said at her frown. 'He doesn't mind. Eddie isn't into serious relationships either.'

'I'm not into *any* sort of relationships!'

He quirked his eyebrow again. 'Bad love affair?' he asked softly.

Sara gave a scornful snort. 'No affair, and no love either. What it was was just bad.'

'And it's over now?'

'Very much so,' she confirmed vehemently.

'Right, then let's go in and dazzle the crowd.'

'In that case I'd better take this off first.' She whisked the cape off, and her blonde curls cascaded down one shoulder and over the breast, pinned by a comb at the nape.

'Wow!' Pete gasped his appreciation. 'Dazzle is the right word. Come on,' he took her arm, 'I'm going to enjoy this.'

Sara walked beside him into the entrance hall of the house. 'Do I really look like this Marie Lindlay? My aunt and—no, just my aunt, she thinks that it's probably just superficial.'

'Well, I hope you don't have Marie's nature. She can be a bit of a flirt on occasion, or so I've heard. But as far as the face and body are concerned you're identical.'

She shook her head. 'It's hard to believe.'

'But true. I looked out some photographs of her today.' He shook his head. 'It's unnatural. Let's go inside, then you can see for yourself.'

The long room they entered was crammed full of people, all of them talking in loud refined voices, and sparkling with diamonds. Several people turned to look at them as the butler showed them in, and a tall redhead broke away from the crowd of people she had been talking to and made her way towards them.

'Our hostess,' Pete had time to mutter before the woman descended on them in an expensive cloud of perfume.

'Peter darling!' she cried before hugging him, kissing him lightly on the cheek. 'And I see you've brought Marie with you.' Her tone cooled somewhat. 'What have you done with Dominic, darling?' she spoke to Sara, her blue eyes hard.

'I——'

'This is Sara Hamille, Cynthia,' Pete interrupted.

The blue eyes became even harder, the beautiful face assessing. 'What game are you playing, Marie?' she finally asked.

Sara looked confused. 'No, really, I——'

'A change of accent doesn't make you any less Marie Lindlay,' the woman scorned. 'And Dominic is going to be furious when he arrives. Oh well,' she said dismissively, 'it's your funeral. Drinks are over there,' she waved her hand vaguely in the direction of the bar. 'Help yourselves to food.' She moved gracefully back to the people she had previously been conversing with.

'You see?' Pete dragged Sara over to the bar. 'If you can fool Cynthia, you can fool anyone. She and Marie have been friends since boarding-school.'

Sara grimaced. 'Are you sure "friends" is the right description?'

'They're like that in this crowd,' he dismissed. 'They stab each other in the back every opportunity they get. For instance, they're probably all looking forward to the scene between Dominic Thorne and the supposed Marie Lindlay.'

'How nice!' she said with unconcealed sarcasm.

'Come on, let's have a drink,' Pete encouraged. 'We might as well enjoy ourselves now we're here.'

An hour later, when Dominic Thorne and Marie Lindlay still hadn't put in an appearance, Sara was beginning to wonder if they were coming, and she said as much to Pete.

'Don't worry,' he assured her gaily, 'they'll be here. It's only just gone ten o'clock.'

'I wouldn't mind,' she grimaced. 'But everyone here seems to think I really am Marie Lindlay. A couple of people have turned nasty because I refuse to admit to being her.'

'Then they're going to get a shock when the real one walks in. Have another drink.'

She was beginning to think they should leave. It was all turning out to be very embarrassing, these people convinced she was the other girl trying to make a fool of them, so much so that she was even beginning to doubt herself. Cynthia Robotham-James, their hostess, had become very annoyed with her a few minutes ago when she had again insisted her name was Sara Hamille.

'Here we go,' Pete suddenly whispered in her ear. 'Look over at the door,' he said fiercely.

Sara looked. Dominic Thorne was instantly recognisable in black velvet jacket and matching trousers, his snowy white shirt emphasising his tan. She held her breath as her gaze passed down to the girl at his side, gasping at what she saw. The hairstyle was different, the dress even more daring than the one she was wearing—if that were possible, and yet looking at the girl at Dominic Thorne's side was like seeing a mirror image. No wonder everyone kept insisting she was Marie. The two of them looked exactly alike!

'You see?' Pete said excitedly. 'Didn't I tell you? Let's go over there.'

'No!' She hung back, too confused at the moment to actually meet the other girl.

'Come on,' Pete insisted. 'I'm not going to miss out on the fun now.'

Sara allowed herself to be pulled towards the doorway, too numb at the moment to offer any resistance. How could two people possibly be so much alike unless they were related in some way, and yet she had no cousins and was an only child herself. She shook her head dazedly, then looked up to find steely blue eyes fixed on her.

Dominic Thorne registered her appearance with a narrowing of those eyes, his body tensing. He looked down at his fiancée and then back to Sara, frowning darkly. He bent down to whisper something in Marie's ear, and she lifted her head, her eyes the same deep brown as Sara's as the two girls stared at each other.

Pete was the only one in the group of four who remained immune to the sudden tension. 'Hi,' he greeted Marie brightly. 'Permit me to introduce Sara Hamille.' He made the announcement with a great deal of pleasure, obviously enjoying this situation immensely.

'Miss Hamille,' Dominic Thorne was the first to break the silence, his voice just as deep and attractive as Sara remembered it, all of him just as attractive as she remembered.

'Mr Thorne,' she acknowledged, still staring at Marie Lindlay, and the other girl stared right back.

Suddenly that beautiful face broke into a smile, a mischievous smile. 'So you're the girl who's been going around London impersonating me?' she accused jokingly.

'Hardly impersonating,' Dominic Thorne replied, completely in control of himself again, *and* the situation. 'Miss Hamille has been acting as herself, it's others who have taken her to be you.' He looked at Sara with narrowed eyes. 'I believe I owe you an apology,' he said, as if the words didn't come easily to him, as if he rarely had to admit to being in the wrong.

'Let's move away from the doorway,' Marie suggested lightly. Her voice was completely different from Sara's, her education obviously having been in one of England's finest boarding-schools. 'We're attracting a lot of attention standing here.'

'I'm afraid that's my fault,' Sara admitted as they moved to a less prominent part of the room. 'The people here refused to believe I wasn't Marie Lindlay, and now that you've arrived . . .' she shrugged.

'Ooh, how lovely!' Marie clapped her hands in delight. 'Isn't this fun, Dominic?' she exclaimed.

'I doubt Miss Hamille has thought it so, it can't have been easy being thought to be you,' he added dryly.

'Oh, Dominic!' Marie pouted prettily.

He turned to look at Sara, his eyes once again registering his shock at her likeness to his fiancée. 'I really must apologise for my behaviour yesterday evening.' His voice was stilted, his manner haughty. 'You must have thought me very strange.'

Sara flushed. 'And you must have thought me even stranger.'

'Not really,' he shook his head.

Marie gave a tinkling laugh, her long blonde hair brushed free about her shoulders. 'Dominic has this mad idea that I keep going off with other men.' She looked up at him through dark, silky, lashes. 'Don't you, my jealous darling?'

Sara found Marie's clinging behaviour where Dominic Thorne was concerned rather uncomfortable to watch. The reason for this feeling was easily explained; it was like watching herself—and she knew she could never act that way with this arrogant man.

But maybe Dominic Thorne had reason to be suspicious of Marie. The man in Soho had certainly been more than a friend to her.

'I'm sure Miss Hamille isn't interested in what I do or do not think,' he said curtly. 'Now don't you think we should make our presence known to Cynthia?'

It was a deliberate snub, but not one Marie seemed about to endorse. 'I can't lose sight of my double now. Just think of the fun we could have, Sara,' her eyes lit up with pleasure. 'We could play some terrific tricks on people!' She turned Sara towards the mirror that adorned the wall behind them. 'It's incredible,' she said breathlessly, staring at their reflections.

And it was incredible, the likeness was uncanny. Sara's hair was possibly a little lighter in colour, bleached by years under the Florida sun, and her skin was a more golden colour against Marie's magnolia colouring, but other than that they were identical—the same height, the same features, even the same slender fingers, but a huge diamond ring sparkled on the third finger of Marie's left hand.

'I think unbelievable is a more apt word.' Dominic Thorne came to stand between them. 'Have you always looked like this, Miss Hamille?' The question was almost an accusation.

She flushed at his tone. 'Are you implying I've had

plastic surgery to make me look like Marie? Because I can assure you I haven't,' she said indignantly.

'No, she hasn't,' Pete cut in, indignant on her behalf. 'I can spot that sort of thing a mile away. Sara was born with that face.'

'Well, I can assure you *I* haven't had plastic surgery, Dominic,' Marie told her fiancé.

'Considering I've known you since you were ten years old I would say that was obvious,' he scorned. 'But there has to be some explanation for this.'

'I can't think of one,' Marie dismissed. 'Come on, Sara, we'll go and show Cynthia you aren't a liar at all.' She took Sara by the arm and led her away.

Sara was fuming, aware of the fact that Dominic Thorne didn't like her, distrusted her. Plastic surgery indeed!

'You mustn't mind Dominic.' Marie seemed to read her thoughts. 'He's suspicious by nature.'

Sara couldn't dismiss him so easily, although she did her best as Marie led her from group to group, the other girl loving the sensation they were causing.

'I really must get back to Pete,' Sara insisted at last, having noticed that he was having extreme difficulty conversing with the taciturn Dominic Thorne, those steely blue eyes never leaving Marie and herself.

Marie looked regretful. 'And I suppose I should get back to Dominic.' The smile she gave him was radiant, her hand once again through the crook of his arm as she looked up at him affectionately.

'I think we should be going now,' Sara told Pete.

'Surely not?' To her surprise it was Dominic Thorne who made the objection. 'I was just going to ask you if you would care to dance.'

Sara loved to dance, although Pete had assured her that he was absolutely tone deaf and so hopeless at dancing. But despite her love of dancing she didn't relish the idea of being relatively alone with Dominic Thorne.

'I really think we should be leaving now.' She put as

much regret in her voice as she could in the circum-
stances.

Those hard blue eyes remained fixed on her face. 'One
dance isn't going to delay you too long, surely?' he persisted.

'I——'

'Oh, go on, Sara,' Pete encouraged. 'Five minutes isn't
going to make that much difference.'

'It never pays to argue with Dominic,' even Marie
added her argument in favour of the dance.

Sara gave a resigned shrug. 'Very well, I'd love to
dance, Mr Thorne.'

'Dominic, please,' he could be heard saying as he
manoeuvred her on to the space that had been cleared
for dancing, some of the couples around them doing
more than dancing as the alcohol they had consumed
hit their bloodstream. Sara was quite embarassed by
some of the things that were going on. 'Ignore them,'
Dominic advised, seeing her shocked expression.

'I—That's a little difficult,' she gasped as she saw one
man blatantly touching the bare breast of his dancing
partner.

Dominic saw it too, not bothering to dance any more
but taking her hand and leading her out of the double
doors that led to the garden.

Sara snatched her hand away, eyeing him warily. 'Is
it always like that?' she asked disgustedly.

'It gets worse,' he derided.

Then thank goodness she was leaving. And thank
goodness she hadn't actually got to dance with this man.
Even in the brief moment he had pulled her into his
arms she had been aware of his masculinity, of the sensual air that surrounded him. Not that she felt any safer
completely alone with him out here, where the noise of
the party sounded strangely muted. And she soon
realised why—he had closed the doors behind them.

He took a packet of cigars out of his breast pocket,
lighting one with a gold lighter. 'You've obviously never

been to one of Cynthia's parties before,' he mocked.

Sara moved restlessly, wishing he would stop staring at her with those curiously intent eyes, as if he were trying to see into her very soul. 'No,' she confirmed nervously.

'Have you been in England long?' The query sounded casual, and yet Sara had the feeling it wasn't any such thing.

She shrugged. 'A few days.'

He nodded. 'Are you here with your parents?'

'They were both killed in a car accident six months ago,' she said jerkily.

'I see. I'm sorry,' he added as an afterthought. 'So you're over here on holiday?'

'Yes.' No point in mentioning that she was slowly recovering from her own injuries in the car accident, it wasn't of interest to this man.

'So Mr Glenn is a relatively new acquaintance?'

'Very new.' She frowned. 'I don't understand the reason for these questions, Mr Thorne.'

He shrugged. 'You didn't seem surprised by Marie's likeness to you, and as you are obviously an American and have only just arrived in England I wondered how you'd learnt of Marie's existence.'

Sara stiffened. 'I'm not sure that I like your tone, Mr Thorne.' He sounded almost accusing, as if he suspected her of something but hadn't yet stated these suspicions.

'I'm sorry if you take exception to what I've said.' But he didn't look in the least sorry; his expression was hard, his eyes narrowed to icy slits. 'But I'm sure you can understand my puzzlement as to your reason for seeking out my fiancée.'

'I didn't seek her out!' Sara snapped resentfully. 'I admit that I wanted to see her, but only because so many people had taken me to be her, yourself included,' she added pointedly. 'I had no ulterior motive for meeting Marie, as you seem to be implying I have.'

Dominic Thorne remained unmoved by her heated

outburst. 'Did I do that?' he asked silkily.

'You know you did. Just why do *you* think I wanted to see Marie?' There were two spots of angry colour in her cheeks.

He shrugged. 'She's rich, and——'

He didn't get any further. Sara's hand swung up to strike him forcibly on the side of the face, and she watched with satisfaction as angry red welts appeared on his rigid cheek. This satisfaction soon faded as she saw the angry glitter in glacial blue eyes.

'You deserved that!' she spluttered, backing away. 'You——'

Now it was his turn to render her speechless—only his method was much more destructive! Barry had liked to kiss her, in his practised way he had believed he was arousing her, but this man, Dominic Thorne, ravaged her mouth with his lips, bent her curves to mould against his hard muscled body, rendered her breathless—and aroused her against her will.

'How dare you!' she demanded when he at last released her mouth, pushing away from him.

Her indignation only served to amuse him. 'Couldn't you have come out with something a little more original than that?' he mocked. 'You disappoint me, Miss Hamille.'

Her eyes flashed. 'And you disappoint me too, Mr Thorne!' She wiped her mouth with the back of her hand, watching his expression darken. 'I had expected more than brutality from the celebrated Dominic Thorne,' she added insultingly.

'You know,' he drawled slowly, 'your similarity to Marie is only skin-deep.' His look was contemptuous of her slender curves and flushed face.

'Maybe she appreciates your—your savagery,' she spat the words at him angrily, 'but I don't! Excuse me, Mr Thorne, I hope I never have the misfortune to meet you again.' She spun on her heel, but was stopped from leaving by his hand on her arm. 'Let go of me!' she ordered coldly.

He looked down at her, his jaw rigid, a pulse beating rapidly in his throat. 'I hope we never meet again, Sara,' his voice was husky. 'But for a completely different reason from yours.'

'Goodbye, Mr Thorne!' She swung away from him, and this time he made no effort to stop her.

'Goodbye, Sara . . .' he said softly as she closed the door behind her.

She marched straight over to Pete as he still stood talking to Marie, her anger making her look even more beautiful in that moment. 'I'm ready to leave,' she told Pete tautly.

Marie burst out laughing. 'Has Dominic been upsetting you?' she chuckled. 'I can see he has.' She put her arm through Sara's. 'You mustn't mind Dominic. If he's been insulting you, which I think he must have done, he was probably only trying to protect me. Dominic always thinks he has to protect me from something.'

'Then this time he's done a good job of it,' Sara said distantly. 'I'm sorry I bothered you, Miss Lindlay. I can assure you I had no intention of upsetting you in any way.'

Marie's smile was openly scornful. 'I'm not upset. I've had the most fun tonight that I've had in a long time. If you give me your telephone number perhaps I can call you some time and we can have lunch together.'

Sara hesitated, Dominic Thorne's determination for Marie and herself never to meet again fixed firmly in her mind. He had made his opinion more than clear, and she doubted if many people opposed that strong will of his.

'Oh, please do,' Marie encouraged. 'Dominic doesn't even have to know about it. Please,' she added with a beguiling smile.

Sara knew this sort of persuasion of old—she must look exactly the same when she tried to get her own way. How could she possibly refuse! 'All right.' She wrote out her aunt's telephone number on the piece of paper Marie provided. 'But I'm only here for another couple of weeks at the most.'

'Oh, I'll call you before then,' Marie assured her.

Sara saw Dominic Thorne fast approaching their little group and so she hurriedly made her goodbyes. She had had enough of him for one evening.

'Where did Thorne take you?' Pete asked on the drive home.

'Outside,' she revealed furiously. 'He seemed to think I was trying to pull a stunt on them.'

Pete laughed. 'Men like him don't understand coincidence. How did you like Marie?' he gave her a sideways glance.

'How did *you* like her?' She quirked an eyebrow at him. She hadn't missed their slightly flirtatious manner when she had rejoined them.

'I liked her a lot,' he acknowledged softly. 'It's strange, the two of you look exactly alike, and yet there's a difference. You have an air of sexual challenge about you that Marie doesn't have, and I'm into the innocent look at the moment. Not that I'm complaining,' he added hastily, 'but I think Thorne probably spends most of his time fighting men off her.'

'He certainly watches over her well,' Sara said moodily.

'So would I,' Pete grinned.

'Lecherous beast!' She started to relax a little, her indignation about Dominic Thorne's treatment of her put firmly to the back of her mind. 'I doubt if Marie would stay innocent for long around you.'

He shrugged. 'Marie has these vibrations ... and I felt them.'

Sara gave him a worried look. 'I wouldn't advise stepping on those particular toes.' Dominic Thorne would deal far more ruthlessly with a man.

'If the lady's willing ...'

'Ah, but is she?'

'I think she could be,' he nodded.

She shrugged. 'Then I wish you luck.'

If Dominic Thorne found out about it then Pete was going to need more than luck!

Her aunt and uncle were already in bed when she got in, although her aunt called to her as she changed into her nightclothes. Her uncle was fast asleep, but her aunt had her own bedside lamp on and had been reading. She put the book down when Sara came quietly into the room.

'Oh, don't mind your uncle,' her aunt said at her questioning look. 'He can sleep through anything, and often does. Did you have a nice time, dear?'

'Quite nice, thank you.' But she wouldn't be seeing Pete again. They had parted as friends, but he was just another man who found Marie more attractive; Dominic Thorne had already made it known that she in no way compared to his Marie. 'I'm not seeing Pete again, he's going to be very busy the next few weeks,' she excused to her aunt.

'Were they nice people at this party?'

Sara smiled. 'Or slightly mad like Pete?' she teased.

'Yes,' her aunt admitted guiltily.

'They were all—very nice.'

'Well, I'm glad you had an enjoyable evening.' She plumped up her pillow. 'I think I'll go to sleep now that I know you're home.'

' 'Night,' and Sara quietly left the room.

For some reason she had been loath to mention her meeting with Dominic Thorne and Marie Lindlay to her aunt.

CHAPTER THREE

EDDIE wanted to know all about her evening when he took her for her drive the next day.

'Was Marie Lindlay really. like you?' he asked her.

She smiled. 'Pete didn't think so, he found her infinitely more attractive.'

'The man has no taste!' Eddie scoffed.

'Marie's fiancé seemed to agree with him.'

'Thorne? Well, I suppose he does—after all, he's going to marry her.'

'Yes.'

Eddie quirked an eyebrow. 'You don't sound too sure?'

'Oh, I'm sure they'll marry. It's just that—well, they're an odd couple. Dominic Thorne must be years older than her, for one thing.'

He shrugged. 'Thirty-five isn't old.'

'On him it is!'

Eddie laughed. 'He certainly hasn't made a conquest out of you.'

'Does he usually?' Sara scorned.

'Has them queueing up,' Eddie nodded. 'Before his engagement to Marie Lindlay this last year he was the most sought after man in town. Come to think of it,' he grinned, 'he still is.'

'Mm, he doesn't look the faithful type.' He had been a man completely in command, who did what he wanted when he wanted, and woe betide anyone who got in his way. Besides, he hadn't hesitated about kissing her.

'Then they make a good pair,' Eddie said dryly.

Sara gave him a sharp look. 'Meaning?'

'Meaning Pete has a date with the lovely Marie this evening.'

She couldn't hide her surprise. Dominic Thorne would be furious about that if he ever found out. And why on earth was Marie doing it? Having seen for herself how angry Dominic Thorne had been when he had thought *she* was Marie out with Eddie, then Sara thought Marie ought to have more sense. After all, she must know him so much better than Sara did, must realise the full force of his anger—and the full force of his love-making too! No one seemed to wait for the wedding any more.

Except Sara! Barry had constantly tried to persuade her into a more intimate relationship, and she had always refused, something she was glad of when he let her down in that way. How much more awful it would have been if they had been lovers!

There was such a lot of pressure about sex nowadays, from television, advertising, and most of all from society itself. Sara had been thought something of a freak by her model friends because she had no tales of bedroom romps to tell them.

They had found great pleasure in recounting whose bed they had slept in—although from all accounts sleep was the last thing they did!—the evening before, and although Sara had politely listened she had found it all rather sordid, instead of the excitement the other girls insisted it was.

Not that she was a prude, and she certainly didn't say to herself before she went out with a man, 'I must not sleep with him'; she just hadn't ever met a man that she loved, a man who excited her so much she gave herself to him willingly. If that day ever came she would go to him without thought of the future, would give herself body and soul into his keeping.

What her friends in the States didn't seem to realise was that they were invited out for the evening, perhaps two evenings, and when these men had taken the thing they were really interested in they didn't want to know any more.

'Hey, you weren't interested in Pete yourself, were you?' Eddie broke into her thoughts.

'No,' she could deny with ease. 'I was just wondering why Marie took such risks.'

He shrugged. 'For the hell of it, I should think. Thorne must be something to see in a jealous rage.'

Not really. He had treated *her* more like a naughty schoolgirl when he had ordered her home from the casino. And he hadn't taken her home himself, but had told her to get her escort to take her. Not exactly a jealous rage!

'Is it almost lunchtime?' she changed the subject. 'I'm starting to get very hungry.'

Eddie grinned. 'I thought you'd never ask! I don't mind being your chauffeur, but all this green countryside and pure fresh air is making me thirsty.'

Sara felt very guilty, because she had hardly noticed the countryside she had come out to see, being much too wrapped up in thoughts of Dominic Thorne and Marie Lindlay. Not that she ever expected to hear from the other girl; she felt sure her arrogant fiancé would make sure that she didn't.

'Where are we?' she asked with interest.

'Royal Berkshire,' he announced.

'Oh? Anywhere near Windsor Castle?'

Eddie grimaced. 'Very near. Don't tell me you want to see that too?'

'Well ... I wouldn't mind.' She gave him a coaxing smile.

'Okay,' he sighed. 'But a beer and lunch first,' he added as her face lit up with excitement.

'Lunch in a pub?' Her eyes glowed. 'Oh, good,' she grinned. 'I'm really getting to like your English pubs.'

Eddie drove into a pub car park. 'For goodness' sake don't tell Aunt Susan I've taken you to another one. She gave me an earful the last time!'

'I won't tell her,' Sara assured him.

It seemed there were a lot of things she was keeping to herself lately, and not normally being a secretive girl she was surprised at herself.

Lunch was delicious, a lovely prawn salad served to them out in the garden. Sara also enjoyed the lager and lime Eddie bought her. She enjoyed going around Windsor Castle too, and although Eddie moaned about it she thought he secretly enjoyed it too.

'I bet it's years since you went there,' she teased on the drive home. The time was now well on the way towards dinner.

Eddie looked shamefaced. 'Well, actually, I—I've never been before,' he admitted.

Her eyes widened. 'Never been to Windsor Castle?'

'There's no need to look so surprised.' He looked sheepish. 'It isn't unusual not to visit a place that's more or less on your doorstep. You've probably never been to Disney World!' he scorned.

'Wrong,' Sara smiled. 'I've been dozens of times—I love it. It's absolutely fantastic. I feel like a little girl again when I go there.'

'You probably look like one too. You're very easy to be with, Sara,' Eddie said suddenly. 'And I mean that in the nicest way possible.'

'I know,' she accepted huskily. 'I've enjoyed today.'

'So have I.' He seemed surprised by the fact.

'It's just like having a brother,' she said sleepily, leaning tiredly back against the headrest.

'It's okay,' Eddie laughed, 'I wasn't moving in for the kill.'

Sara smiled at her own conceit, then dozed off in the warmth of the car and the monotonous hum of the engine.

She woke with a jerk, a curious feeling of foreboding hanging over her.

The feeling persisted over the next few days, so much so

that she found she wasn't sleeping at night. The doctor had warned her of this delayed shock, the long air flight on top of her already weakened state sapping what little energy she had, and she spent the next three or four days resting, not going far from the house.

Consequently she was at home when Marie Lindlay telephoned her, and answered the call herself. The idea of meeting for lunch appealed to her, and the two girls arranged to meet at a restaurant in town.

There was no sign of Marie when she arrived at the arranged time, although the doorman insisted on calling *her* 'Miss Lindlay'. Sara found the situation too complicated to explain, leaving him under the misapprehension that she really was Marie. The poor man would think himself intoxicated when Marie did arrive.

She came into the restaurant twenty minutes later, and the first five minutes of their conversation were taken up with her apologies.

'It was Dominic,' she sighed, ordering a Bacardi and Coke from the hovering waiter. 'Whenever Daddy's away he seems to think he has to keep checking up on me. It's nonsense, of course, but he still does it. He kept me on the telephone ten minutes trying to find out where I was going.'

'When are you getting married?' Sara asked, wondering what she was doing here now that she was actually here.

'Oh, not for ages yet,' Marie dismissed, nodding at the waiter as he put her drink on the table. 'Dominic's in no hurry, and neither am I.'

'But surely you've been engaged for almost a year,' Sara frowned, not seeing Dominic Thorne as the patient type.

'Just under six months,' Marie corrected. 'And to tell you the truth, I'm not sure I'd be very good as a wife for Dominic. He's such a perfectionist.'

Sara smiled. 'I'm sure he would make allowances for a new wife.'

'Maybe,' Marie dropped the subject. 'I love your accent. Where in America do you come from?'

Sara told her, also explaining about the accident that had killed her parents and injured her. She found it so easy to talk to the other girl, and Marie seemed to feel the same.

'How sad!' Marie looked genuinely upset. 'I hate death,' she shuddered. 'My mother's dead too.'

'I'm sorry.'

Marie seemed to shake off her dark mood, and gave a dazzling smile. 'Let's order lunch.'

Sara was amazed at the other girl's capacity for passing from topic to topic, from mood to mood, and it seemed that during lunch they discussed every subject possible. By the end of the meal Sara felt that they were friends.

'I still can't get over our likeness,' said Marie as they went from the restaurant into the lounge for coffee. 'Dominic's convinced it's all a trick on your part,' she giggled.

Sara stiffened. 'I'm well aware of your fiancé's opinion of me.'

'And he's aware of yours,' Marie grinned. 'Did you really hit him?'

Sara kept her eyes down on her coffee cup. 'Did he say I had?'

'He didn't need to, it was pretty obvious. God, he was in a foul temper the rest of the evening! I've never seen him in such a black mood.' Marie didn't seem perturbed by the fact, grinning widely.

'He deserved it,' Sara said tightly.

'I'm sure he did,' Marie nodded. 'The trouble with Dominic is that he's perfect himself, and he expects others to be the same.' She shrugged. 'I'm afraid that even I don't meet up to his high standards.'

That Dominic Thorne made her feel totally inadequate was obvious, and that Marie admired him tremendously was also obvious.

'Dominic thinks you're trying to get money out of me in some way,' Marie added guilelessly. 'Or Daddy.'

Sara frowned. 'But I've never met your father, nor have I made any effort to contact him.'

'No,' Marie grinned. 'But Dominic thinks my father may have met your mother, about nine months before you were born.'

An angry tide of red colour passed in front of Sara's eyes. Dominic Thorne had a disgusting mind. How dared he imply that about her mother!

Marie laughed at her expression. 'Don't worry, I soon disabused him of that—my father was devoted to my mother. That's the reason he's never re-married.'

'And my mother loved my father. Your fiancé really does have a twisted mind! Besides, I didn't make any effort to see you again, and if I'd been up to something underhand surely I would have done?'

'Dominic says that was just a clever move on your part,' Marie shrugged.

Sara drew in an angry breath. 'Your fiancé says altogether too much!'

'Actually, he doesn't,' Marie said seriously. 'He doesn't talk much at all, but when he does you can bet it's something important. Now I'm the opposite, I chatter on for hours and none of it makes much sense.'

Sara had already noticed that, and she liked it. She liked Marie too, found her bubbly, flamboyant nature the complete opposite of her own more reserved one.

She considered they had talked about Dominic Thorne quite enough for one day. 'What do you do?' she asked Marie.

'For a living, you mean?' Marie sounded scandalised.

Sara laughed at her expression. 'By your reaction I take it you don't do anything.'

'Is that terribly naughty of me?' Marie looked like a guilty little girl.

'No,' Sara smiled. 'I wish I could do the same.' Although she wasn't sure she really meant that. Her months of enforced inactivity had made her long to go back to work, although she accepted that the injuries to her legs had made it impossible for her to do anything too strenuous. But nevertheless she didn't think she would enjoy being idle. Her mother and father had been quite well off, and that money had now been left to her, but she had never been encouraged to sit at home and live off that wealth. Even her mother had been her stepfather's chief assistant at the advertising agency.

'I'm kept quite busy,' Marie told her. 'Daddy's always entertaining, and I have to be his hostess. And then there's the sports club, I go there a lot. And then——'

'Okay, okay,' Sara laughingly silenced her, 'I believe you!'

'You're a model, aren't you?' Marie said interestedly. 'Pete told me,' she explained.

'Oh yes.' Sara bit her lip, undecided about saying anything to Marie about her date with Pete. After all, it was none of her business who the other girl went out with. And yet ... 'Did you have a nice evening with him?' she queried.

Marie shrugged. 'He's okay. I—Hey, I didn't step on any toes, did I? He told me there was nothing between the two of you,' she frowned.

'There isn't. I wasn't thinking of me.' Sara quirked one eyebrow.

'Then who——? Oh, you mean Dominic,' the other girl dismissed. 'Mm, I don't suppose he would like it much.'

'He would have a right not to. You are engaged to him,' Sara gently reminded her.

'He's kept very busy, he works very hard. And then

he's often away on business. I get very lonely. Anyway, I won't be seeing Pete again.'

That didn't particularly bother her. Marie could have a hundred other men besides Dominic Thorne if she wanted to, but she had the feeling that he wouldn't stand too much of that treatment, and unless Marie wanted to lose him she would have to curb her activities with other men.

Marie didn't seem to agree with her when she pointed that out to her. 'He'll forgive me,' she dismissed lightly. 'He always has.'

Then Dominic Thorne must be a more understanding man than she would have given him credit for. Maybe he loved Marie more deeply than he appeared to on the surface. He was definitely a deep character.

'My marriage to Dominic will make things all neat and tidy,' Marie told her, at her frowning look. 'He and my father are partners, you see. When we marry Dominic is assured of eventually becoming sole owner. He's been so good to me, it's the least I can do for him. And he's so gorgeous, isn't he? So distinguished.'

'Yes.' Although marrying him because he had been good to her didn't seem a very good reason to Sara. Perhaps they loved each other in their own way, but it wasn't the way she wanted to love her life's partner.

'Mm, I love to be seen with him.' Marie's expression was dreamy. 'And he's so masterful. Daddy says he's a brilliant businessman.'

Sara hastily revised her opinion of Marie not loving her fiancé. She obviously adored him, although she took pains to hide it. Their relationship was too complicated for her to understand, so she decided not to probe any further. The two of them obviously understood each other, and really that was all that mattered.

'I—Oh, look, there's Suzanne,' Marie exclaimed. 'Suz—Oh, damn, she's gone into the restaurant.' She turned to Sara. 'Would you mind if I left you for a few minutes? I just have to see Suzanne.'

'No,' Sara smiled. 'You go ahead.'

Marie stood up, hesitating. 'You won't leave?'

She shook her head. 'No, I won't leave. I'll finish drinking my coffee and wait for you here.'

Marie was gone considerably longer than a few minutes, so much so that Sara started to get fidgety. When she saw Dominic Thorne enter the restaurant her heart sank. Verbal abuse from him was not something she welcomed right now, not after the things Marie had told her he had said about her, the insults he had made about both her and her mother.

He came straight over to her, his strides long and purposeful. 'I thought I'd find you here.' He stood looking down at her. 'Why couldn't you have told me earlier instead of all that evasion?' He sat down in the chair Marie had recently vacated, his dark suit impeccable, as was the rest of his appearance.

He thought she was Marie! Her anger at his accusations concerning her mother and herself came to the fore. She tried to recall Marie's husky tone of voice, hoping she could pull this off. This man was arrogant, condescending, and totally wrong about her, and it was time she got her own back on him.

'Maybe I didn't want you breathing down my neck.' Was that really her talking? She had managed to get quite a good impression of Marie's husky tones, good enough to fool Dominic Thorne, she could tell.

He sighed, his anger barely contained. 'I merely like to know——'

'—What I'm doing every minute of the day and night,' she finished in that highly educated English voice. Maybe she should take up acting? 'I'm only out to lunch, Dominic.'

He put his hand over hers, and Sara only just stopped herself from pulling away. 'I feel responsible for you while your father is away.'

Sara pouted as she had seen Marie do. 'But, Dominic, surely I can't come to any harm while I'm out to lunch?'

He gave an indulgent smile, looking the most pleasant she had ever seen him, his harshly attractive features softened. 'You could come to harm just sitting at home,' he teased. 'Who are you lunching with?'

'Well, actually——'

Dominic's face darkened, his eyes narrowed to icy blue slits. 'You haven't seen the Hamille girl again, have you?'

Sara bristled angrily on her own behalf. 'And why shouldn't I?' Amazingly she still managed to maintain Marie's accent.

'I've already told you why,' he said sternly. 'The girl is out to cause trouble.'

As far as Sara was concerned this charade had gone on long enough! 'And in what way am I doing that, Mr Thorne?' She dropped the pose, talking to him in her own voice, her anger obvious.

He instantly dropped her hand, his face an angry mask. 'Very amusing, Miss Hamille,' he snapped. 'Perhaps you should take up acting as a profession.'

Her mouth twisted. 'I had just thought the same thing. Let me assure you, Mr Thorne, I am not out to cause "trouble". I met Marie today at her suggestion, and because I like her. But now that I know your opinion of my mother and myself—and incidentally, my mother didn't meet Marie's father at any time, let alone nine months before my birth. I'm sorry, Mr Thorne, did you say something?' she asked coldly.

His expression was fierce. 'I said damn Marie and her loose tongue,' he rasped.

'If the remarks hadn't been made she wouldn't have been able to repeat them. Twenty-one years ago my mother was married to my father, and that is the time I was born. The comments you made about her are slanderous,' her eyes sparkled with fury, 'and I'm not going to sit back and let you make them!'

'It was merely conjecture,' he said smoothly. 'Your similarity to Marie is—amazing. I was merely trying to find a reason for it.'

'Well, that isn't it!' Sara snapped.

'No, I accept that. Your age would seem to veto that idea. Twenty-one, I think you said?'

'Almost,' she confirmed resentfully. 'Next month.'

'Mm, and at the time Marie's father was also happily married to her mother.'

'I require an apology for your remarks, Mr Thorne,' Sara told him stubbornly.

Anger flared in those narrowed eyes. 'Miss Hamille——'

'An apology!' she repeated tightly. 'My mother is dead and so unable to defend herself, but I demand an apology on her behalf.' She looked at him challengingly, refusing to withdraw from their silent optical battle. Marie might enjoy his domineering attitude, but Sara just found it infuriating, and she refused to be cowed by it.

Dominic Thorne looked as if he were going through a battle of his own, with himself. That he was unaccustomed to admitting to being wrong about anything she had no doubt, but she remained firm. He *would* apologise.

'All right,' the words came out in a hiss, blue eyes glittering resentfully. 'I apologise. It would appear I'm mistaken.'

Sara could thankfully see Marie coming back, the other girl bending to lightly kiss her fiancé on the lips before sitting down beside him.

'Sorry I was so long,' she spoke to Sara. 'I'm afraid Suzanne is as much of a chatterbox as I am!' She gave a glowing smile in Dominic Thorne's direction. 'What are you doing here, darling? Not that I'm not pleased to see you,' she entwined her fingers with his, 'but I thought you'd be hard at work this afternoon.'

'I had some spare time.' His voice showed none of his fury of seconds earlier, his manner at once indulgent. 'I thought I might find you here.'

So that he could spy on her, Sara silently fumed. And it seemed that Dominic Thorne loved Marie in return, a possessive over-protective love that would suffocate Sara.

'Sara and I are going shopping,' Marie surprised her by announcing. 'Do you want to come with us?' she asked her fiancé.

'No, thanks,' he gave a teasing smile. 'But you can show me later what you bought.'

Marie gave him a mischievous smile. 'I thought I might buy some lingerie.'

Dominic laughed, at once sensually attractive. 'In that case you can definitely show it to me later!' He stood up. 'I'll leave you two girls to enjoy your shopping.'

'Goodbye, Mr Thorne,' Sara said pointedly, meeting his sharp look unflinchingly.

He nodded curtly. 'Goodbye, Miss Hamille. Until later, Marie,' and he bent to kiss her, a tall compelling man who drew much attention as he left the restaurant.

Marie gave a pleasurable shiver. 'I don't think I'll ever get over how attractive he is,' she smiled. 'Or the fact that I'm engaged to him. Oh well, shall we go and do that shopping now?'

It was late when Sara got back to her aunt's house, her leavetaking from Marie having been difficult. Marie had wanted them to meet again, but Sara had claimed that she would be too busy during her time left in England.

Marie called her again a couple of days later, and Sara did her best to get out of seeing her.

'Please,' Marie coaxed. 'I like you, Sara, I feel I can talk to you. I know,' her husky laugh sounded down the telephone, 'I never do anything else! But I feel I can *really* talk to you. Maybe it's because we're so much alike, I don't know, but I feel as if there's a bond between us.'

Sara felt it too, so much so that it felt weird. She wasn't even sure that she and Marie had anything in common, she just felt close to the other girl, wanted to help her if she was troubled about anything.

'Oh, go on, Sara,' Marie encouraged, sensing her weakening. 'I'll pick you up, shall I?'

'No!' her voice was sharp. She still hadn't mentioned her first two meetings with Marie to her aunt and uncle, and she didn't want to have to tell them now. 'I—I'll meet you somewhere.'

They arranged a place to meet, and Sara duly turned up there at the appropriate time. Marie was late, but then time never seemed to mean much to her, possibly because she had so much of it on her hands.

After quarter of an hour she was starting to worry, after half an hour she was convinced something had happened to Marie. Luckily the other girl's telephone number was in the book, and she rang through to the house. The maid told her that Miss Lindlay was resting in her room, and that she certainly didn't have an appointment to meet anyone this afternoon.

Sara didn't know what to make of that, standing dazedly in the callbox, until an irate person outside began to knock on the window. She slowly moved out of the callbox, stunned by what she had just been told. It sounded like a brush-off to her, and considering that Marie had been the one who wanted the meeting she didn't think it was her doing. There could be only one person behind this—Dominic Thorne!

She waited until the other person left the callbox before putting a call through to Dominic Thorne's office. Without even asking her name his secretary told her he wasn't available, and would she like to leave a message. What she had to say to Dominic Thorne couldn't be relayed through a third party!

'Could you tell him Sara Hamille called,' she said

stiffly before putting the receiver down.

So that she didn't completely waste her time she went for a walk in one of the parks, amazed that you could find such peace and beauty in the middle of this teeming city.

The fresh air did her good, giving her an appetite for her dinner. She had taken to spending her evenings quietly at home with her aunt and uncle, remaining friends with Eddie but not accepting any more of his invitations. After all, she was here to rest, and she had enough exercise during the day.

She was watching a film on the television when her aunt told her there was a caller for her.

'Take him into the other room,' her aunt said in a whisper. 'It's tidier in there.'

Sara wasn't really surprised by the identity of her caller; he had to be someone quite important for her aunt to suggest using the lounge. Even her aunt had recognised the individualism of Dominic Thorne.

'Yes?' Sara's manner wasn't forthcoming as she fought off feelings of inadequacy. He looked so distinguished in the black evening clothes, showing her denims and tee-shirt up for the casual attire they were.

Dominic Thorne was obviously aware of her clothing too, as his narrowed gaze passed slowly over the length of her body. 'I hope I haven't called at an inconvenient time,' he drawled.

'Not at all.' She put her thumbs through the loops of the waistband of her denims, adopting a challenging stance. 'I'll probably miss knowing who the murderer was after watching the other hour and a half of the film, but what does that matter?' Her sarcasm was unmistakable.

His expression hardened. 'My secretary said you telephoned.'

She raised her eyebrows. 'I didn't expect a personal visit for the call.'

'And you aren't getting one.' His patience seemed to be wearing thin. 'I was in the area and I thought I would come and explain the reason Marie let you down this afternoon.'

'I think I can guess that,' Sara mocked, her head tilted back defiantly.

'I doubt it,' he scowled. 'Marie suffers from migraine. She had one this afternoon.'

'I'm sure!'

Dominic stiffened. 'I am not in the habit of lying.'

Sara's shrug was deliberately provocative. 'Once or twice doesn't make you a habitual liar.'

His hands came out to painfully grasp her arms. 'I'm sure Marie will call you herself tomorrow and explain why she was unable to meet you.'

'I'm sure she will. You've probably instructed her very well.' She was being childish now and she knew it. 'It wasn't my idea that we meet, Mr Thorne. Marie seemed upset about something—and I think I can guess what that something was,' she scorned.

His eyes glittered dangerously as he stood looking down at her, their bodies so close they were almost touching. He shook his head. 'Why did you have to appear in our lives?' he muttered, seeming to be talking to himself, certainly requiring no answer. 'You're a complication I don't need.'

'Don't worry, Mr Thorne,' she snapped. 'Another week and I shall leave as suddenly as I arrived.'

He pushed her away from him. 'I don't think so.'

Sara stepped back, relieved to be away from his blatant masculinity, having found his warm sensuality disturbing in the extreme. He was engaged to be married, it didn't seem fair that he could still command attraction in the way that he did, seemingly without volition.

'Oh, but I shall, Mr Thorne,' she assured him.

'No,' again he shook his head. 'Would you like to see Marie tomorrow?' he asked suddenly.

'I—If she's feeling better,' Sara nodded dazedly.

'She will be,' he said with certainty. 'Well, enough to see you, anyway.' He took out a card, writing on the back of it. 'Come to this address at twelve-thirty tomorrow. It's Marie's home,' he explained as he handed her the card. 'I'm sure she would like to see you for lunch.'

'You're actually encouraging me to see her?'

He shrugged. 'Why not? I'm sure you'll meet anyway, if you want to.'

'Yes.'

'Then come to lunch.'

'Will you be there?'

Dominic smiled, a totally mocking smile. 'I'm afraid so. Has that put you off coming?'

Sara rose to his challenge. 'Certainly not!'

'Very well. Twelve-thirty tomorrow.'

She went with him to the door. 'I'll be there.'

He gave a mocking inclination of his arrogant head, and Sara had to restrain herself from slamming the door after him.

'A friend of yours, dear?' her aunt asked as she rejoined them.

Sara gave a casual shrug. 'Just a friend of a friend,' she dismissed. 'I met him at the club I went to with Eddie the other night,' which was basically true. 'He was in the area and just thought he would call in,' which was also true.

'Nice-looking man,' her aunt remarked.

'Very nice.' If you were partial to arrogant, bossy men! And she wasn't, especially ones who thought themselves omnipotent into the bargain.

She felt hesitant about keeping the luncheon appointment the next day, knowing that her pleasure in seeing Marie had already been dampened by the fact that Dominic Thorne would be there too. She finally decided it would be an act of cowardice not to go. Besides, she didn't even have to speak to Dominic Thorne unless she wanted to.

It seemed he had other ideas about that. As soon as

Sara arrived at the Lindlay house she was shown into what turned out to be a study, and the occupant of that room was none other than Dominic Thorne.

His gaze took in her appearance, the finely checked brown tailored suit and contrasting tan blouse a complete antithesis of her attire of the evening before.

'Marie will be down in a moment—she's still dressing,' he explained her absence.

'Is she feeling better?' Her voice was stilted, distinctly unfriendly.

'Much better. Actually I'm glad she's late, because I have something I wanted to discuss with you.'

'Oh yes?' She was at once on the defensive.

'Yes,' he gave an abrupt nod of his head. 'Please, sit down.' He waited before she had done so before becoming seated himself. 'Now, I'll come straight to the point.' He leant foward over the desk. 'You lied to me, Miss Hamille,' he told her quietly.

Sara's hackles rose indignantly. 'I beg your pardon? I have never at any time lied to you.' Her tone gave the impression that she didn't consider him important enough in her life to bother with such things.

'There is such a thing as lying by omission,' he said coldly. 'I had you checked out, Miss Hamille——'

'You had no right!' Her eyes flashed angrily.

'I had you checked out,' he repeated calmly, 'and I found that your father was not Richard Hamille.'

'I never said he was!'

'Would you kindly let me finish,' Dominic Thorne snapped. 'I also found out that you aren't American by birth, you're English, that——'

The door behind them swung open and another man walked in. Dominic gave Sara a sharp look before greeting the other man.

'You're back early, Michael,' he said almost enquiringly.

'I heard about Marie. I—You aren't Marie!' the man accused, his face paling, going a sickly grey as he continued to look at Sara. 'My God,' he said dazedly, 'if you aren't Marie then you have to be——'

'Sara,' she supplied huskily, feeling as if the world were revolving around her. 'And you're my father!'

The face was much older, the hair greyer, but this man was still the same man her mother had shared her first wedding day with, the man who stood beside her in their wedding photographs, the man her mother had said was dead!

CHAPTER FOUR

THIS was all like some horrendous nightmare. The man standing in front of her couldn't be her father— and yet he was, she knew he was. She had a photograph of him in her handbag somewhere, and although it had been taken twenty-two years ago, on the day of his marriage to her mother, there could be no doubting his identity.

And if this man, Michael Lindlay, was her father, then that made Marie her half-sister. No wonder they were so much alike!

'Sit down,' Dominic instructed as she seemed to pale even more.

She hadn't even been aware of standing up, but she sat down thankfully, staring speechlessly up at her father. He seemed to have been struck dumb too, and the two of them stared at each other in silence.

He was a very distinguished man, tall, with grey wings of colour over his temples, the rest of his hair the same blond as her own and Marie's. His face was handsome, although she guessed him to be in his mid, possibly late, forties. And he looked kind, a touch of sadness in the depth of his brown eyes. Sara found it strange that she should have the same colouring, and look so much like a man she didn't even know.

She turned to Dominic Thorne, to find him watching them warily. 'You knew, didn't you?' she accused huskily.

He shook his head. 'Not at first,' he denied softly.

Michael Lindlay seemed to gather his thoughts together with effort. 'Is this your doing, Dominic?' he demanded to know.

'Not guilty.' Dominic shrugged resignedly. 'I think

you'll find it's not been the conscious act of anyone, just a coincidence.'

Brown eyes narrowed. 'You mean that after all these years Sara just turned up here by accident?'

'Not by accident, but *because* of an accident,' Dominic corrected softly. 'Rachel is dead, Michael. She died six months ago in the same accident that killed her second husband and left Sara badly injured.'

Michael Lindlay swallowed hard. 'Rachel—dead?' he repeated raggedly.

Dominic nodded. 'I'm afraid so.'

He turned to look at Sara. 'Is it true?'

She frowned her puzzlement. 'Yes.'

'Oh God!' her father groaned. 'And you were badly injured. Are you all right now?'

'Yes, thank you,' she answered in a stilted voice, still dazed by this whole affair.

'Did Rach—your mother,' he swallowed hard, 'did she suffer at all?' There was raw pain in his eyes.

Sara shook her head. 'The doctors said not.'

'And Richard?' A certain coolness entered his voice.

'The same,' she answered abruptly. She turned to Dominic Thorne. 'Could you please tell me what's going on? How can my father—Mr Lindlay,' she felt guilty as she saw him wince, 'how can he still be alive when my mother always told me he was dead?'

'For the same reason,' Dominic answered her, 'as Marie was always told her mother was dead.'

Sara gasped. 'Are you saying that my mother was also Marie's mother?'

'I'm saying more than that,' he frowned. 'You still haven't realised, have you?'

Now it was her turn to frown. 'Realised what?'

'That Marie isn't just your sister, but your *twin* sister.'

'No!' she cried, her eyes wide with horror, looking in desperation at her father's grey face. 'That isn't true! Tell me it isn't true,' she pleaded.

He seemed unable to speak, and it was left to Dominic to answer her once again. 'I'm afraid it is true, Sara.'

'But it *can't* be! Tell him,' she grabbed her father's arm. 'Tell him he has it all wrong!'

Michael Lindlay looked at her with tormented eyes. 'But he doesn't, Sara,' he choked, turning away to stare out of the window, his back rigid.

Dominic picked up a sheet of paper from the desk, obviously the report he had received about her. 'I was suspicious from the first,' he told her. 'But I was thrown by the fact that you seemed to be an American. And then there was the fact that you said *both* your parents had been killed in the accident.'

'I always called Richard Dad,' she said stiffly.

Dominic nodded. 'Well, on the basis of those two facts I concluded that your likeness to Marie was just a freak of nature. Then the other day you told me you were twenty-one next month—so is Marie. That was too much of a coincidence for me. Here,' he handed her the report, 'read the last paragraph.'

Sara took it from him. The last paragraph was short and to the point. 'And so we have proved beyond doubt that Sara Hamille is in fact Sara Lindlay, the daughter of Michael Lindlay, and the twin of Marie Lindlay.' Her eyes went to the name printed at the top of the sheet; the reputation of the firm was indisputable. She looked up at her father with an agonised expression, having read the information to herself. 'But why?' she groaned in a choked voice. 'Why did you do it?'

'Here,' Dominic picked up the sheet and held it out to his partner. 'You'd better read this too.'

Michael Lindlay made no effort to take it. 'I can guess what it says,' he said dully, a haunted expression to his face.

Dominic shrugged, dropping the report back on to the desk. 'Then I second Sara's query, why?'

'Why did Rachel take Sara and I take Marie?'

'Exactly!' Sara said bitterly.

Michael drew a ragged breath. 'I think Marie should be here to listen to this,' he sighed. 'I only want to have to say it the once. Will you go and get her, Dominic?'

'Sara?' Dominic frowned at her.

The man she had regarded as her enemy until a few minutes ago now seemed her only hold on reality. 'Don't leave me,' she pleaded, her hand on his arm as she gazed up at him beseechingly.

His breath caught in his throat before his hand came out and grasped hers, his fingers firm and reassuring. 'Maybe you should go and get Marie, Michael,' he suggested quietly, still looking at Sara.

'Of course,' the other man agreed jerkily. 'I—I won't be a moment,' and he closed the door with a decisive click.

Sara swallowed hard, shivering even though the day was warm, and removed her hand from Dominic's. 'I'm sorry,' she told him softly. 'I—I'm just so confused.'

'It's all right,' he reassured her. 'You really thought he was dead, didn't you?'

'Yes. You see, my mother always said—well, she said——'

'Michael's told Marie the same thing about her mother.' He shook his head. 'It's going to take some understanding.'

Sara didn't think she would ever understand the cruelty of separating two babies not yet a year old. Why, she might have gone through her whole life without knowing the bond of her twin. What on earth had possessed her mother and father to do such a thing? She found it cruel in the extreme, and totally incomprehensible.

'But, Daddy,' Marie could be heard complaining as she came into the room, 'I haven't finished my make-up yet. Whatever can be so important that I can't—Sara!' She had turned around and seen her, and her face lit up with pleasure. 'You came!' She came over to take Sara's hand in her own. 'I'm so sorry about yesterday. I have these headaches, you see, and—— But you don't want to hear about that,' a beaming smile banished all thought of yesterday's painful migraine. She turned to look at her father. 'You only had to say Sara was here, Daddy. There was no need to be so mysterious. Don't you think the way we look so alike is just amazing?' She held Sara at her side for her father's opinion.

He was obviously too choked to speak, looking at the two of them in silent wonder.

'Daddy?' Marie prompted impatiently.

'You'll have to excuse your father,' Dominic cut in. 'I'm afraid he's had rather a shock.'

Marie's gaiety instantly left her, and she went to her father's side. 'What is it, Daddy?' she searched his face with a worried frown. 'What's happened?' she asked sharply.

'It's all right, Marie, just calm down,' her father instantly soothed. 'You've just got over one attack, don't bring on another one.' He smoothed her hair back from her face. 'Now, let's all go into the lounge and then we can talk in private—and comfort.'

Michael Lindlay—for Sara couldn't bring herself to call him her father—seemed to have regained his equilibrium, taking control of the situation now that he had himself under control.

'Would you like me to leave, Michael?' Dominic asked him. 'Let you talk to the two girls in private.'

'No!' Sara hadn't meant her protest to be made quite so vehemently, but she couldn't let Dominic go. She needed him.

'She's right,' Michael Lindlay told him. 'You have a right to be here. After all, you're almost a member of this family yourself.'

'What's all this about?' even the lighthearted Marie had sensed the tense atmosphere.

Michael Lindlay bit his bottom lip, obviously having trouble knowing where to start.

'At the beginning, Michael,' Dominic advised him, sitting in one of the armchairs while Marie and Sara sat side by side on the sofa.

'Yes. Yes.' He began pacing the room. 'Rachel and I were very young when we married, only eighteen and nineteen, too young really to know what it was all about. But nevertheless things were going well until Rachel became pregnant.' He sighed. 'We couldn't afford to have a child. I hadn't met your father then, Dominic, and I was still training to be an engineer, living on a pittance. A child was the last thing I needed at that time. But Rachel went into ecstasies about the coming baby, and for a while I think she forgot she had a husband. I'm not proud of what happened next——'

'Another woman?' Sara put in bitterly.

He ran a hand through his grey-blond hair. 'It was a stupid thing to do, stupid and childish. Rachel found out soon after—after the twins were born——'

'Twins?' Marie echoed in an astounded voice. 'Sara and I . . .?' she asked dazedly.

'Yes,' their father nodded.

Marie turned to Sara with glowing eyes. 'You really are my sister?' she said excitedly.

Sara gave a shy smile, not knowing what reaction she had expected from Marie, but it certainly hadn't been such unreserved pleasure. Resentment had been the more expected emotion.

'That's wonderful!' Marie cried happily. 'I've always wanted a sister, but a *twin*——! That's really fantastic!'

Sara wished she could share her sister's questionless enthusiasm, but there was too much she still wanted to know, to try and understand. Unable to answer Marie, she simply took her hand in hers, holding on tightly. 'Go on,' she told her—father.

He drew a ragged breath, a catch in his throat as he looked at the two of them sitting so close together. 'When Rachel found out,' he continued huskily, 'she ended our marriage right then and there, wouldn't have anything to do with me. Oh, we continued to live together, a case of her staying with me for the sake of the children. Then Rachel met Richard,' he swallowed hard. 'He was over here on business, and they fell in love. Rachel wanted to go back to America with him, taking the twins with her. I wouldn't allow that, and she—she wouldn't leave without them. In the end——'

'In the end you compromised!' Sara finished shrilly. 'You parted Marie and myself, took a child each.'

Her father looked at her pleadingly. 'Try to understand——'

'There's nothing *to* understand,' she told him angrily. 'You and my mother selfishly parted my twin and myself, because neither of you wanted to miss out! My God, you disgust me!' Her voice rose to a shout.

'Sara!' Dominic warned. 'Sara, don't!'

She looked at him with tears in her eyes. 'I know you mean well,' she choked. 'But I can't *ever* forget what they did.' She ran to the door. 'I'm sorry, Marie, I'll call you.'

'Sara!' Dominic caught hold of her arm. 'Your father——'

'No!' Her eyes flashed deeply brown. 'Don't ever call him that! Richard was my father. He certainly never hurt me as Mr Lindlay has. Now, please, let me go.'

He looked down at her with compassionate eyes. 'I'll take you home if you want to go. All right?' he said softly.

She frowned, unable to think straight. 'I—No——'

'Yes,' he insisted firmly.

'Shall I come with you?' Marie wanted to know.

'No, stay with your father,' Dominic advised.

'Could we please leave now?' Sara muttered. 'Before I make an absolute fool of myself and faint.'

'Sara——'

'Not now, Michael,' Dominic cut him off harshly. 'Can't you see what you've already done to her?' he said savagely. 'For God's sake don't say any more. Let's get out of here,' he muttered to Sara.

Sara sat miserably hunched up on her side of the

Rolls-Royce, too numb to care where he was driving or where he was taking her. To think that her mother, a woman she had always loved and admired, had committed that atrocity! How could two people do that to innocent children, change their lives so completely before they had even begun?

'I really had no idea,' Dominic broke the silence. 'No idea at all,' he repeated with a shake of his head. 'It seems incredible to think I've known Michael all these years, and all the time he was hiding this secret.'

'I knew my mother all my life,' she said bitterly. 'And I would never have thought her capable of something like this.'

Dominic shrugged. 'She was very young, only your age——'

'You think I could do a thing like that?' she rounded on him angrily.

He gave her a sideways glance. 'No, I don't think you could. But put yourself in her place. Go on, Sara,' he said firmly as she went to protest. 'Right. Now you're married to a man you no longer love, you have two children by him. Suddenly you meet a man you do love, and you want to be with him, but your husband refuses to give up his children. What do you do?'

'I—Why I—He should have let my mother take both of us,' she declared. 'It was pure selfishness——'

'Wasn't it selfish of your mother to want both the children, to take them thousands of miles away? She already had the man she loved, your father was left with nothing.'

'He—I——' she frowned. 'Separating us was not the answer!'

'I agree. But what was? Can you tell me?'

Sara bit her lip. 'No . . .' she finally admitted.

'Your father has suffered for that one lapse in their relationship,' Dominic told her quietly.

'How?' she scorned.

'By loving your mother all these years.'

Sara gasped. 'But he said——'

'Yes?' Dominic quirked one eyebrow. 'Your father never at any time this afternoon said he didn't love your mother. They had a momentary setback because like a lot of young people they wonder how they're going to manage to live when they start a family. It's often a time of great strain. Your mother coped with it by involving herself in plans for the birth of her baby, your father coped with it——'

'By having an affair!'

'By being with a woman who maybe listened to his anxieties——'

'Among other things!'

Dominic sighed. 'I accept that it wasn't a very sensible thing to do, but then human beings aren't infallible. When it was too late to save the marriage or revive your mother's love for him, he realised how much he really loved her. And he's continued to love her. Finding out she's dead hit him very badly.'

Sara turned away, wishing she could feel compassion for her father, but still feeling only resentment. 'How do you know all this?' she finally asked him. 'About him still loving my mother.'

He shrugged. 'Michael's never made any secret of it. Maybe now that she really is dead ... Well, maybe now he'll start to forget. And forgive.'

'My mother——'

'Not your mother, Sara,' he interrupted patiently. 'Himself.'

'Himself . . .?'

'It can't have been easy living with himself all this time. Maybe you should try to forgive too.'

'And maybe you should mind your own damned business,' she snapped. 'You may be going to marry my sister, but that doesn't mean you have any say in how *I* live my life.'

His expression was harsh. 'You can live your life any damn way you please, but when it involves Marie then I have a say in it. She's very fond of you already, and I—I like her to have things that make her happy. *You* make her happy.'

Sara knew that they were engaged, but she hadn't figured on Dominic being that besotted with Marie. He didn't seem the sort of man who would ever allow his emotions to rule his head. He must love Marie very much. And somehow Sara didn't like that idea.

She brought her thoughts up with a start. Somewhere along the line, probably when she had appealed to him for his support, she had become more than a little attracted to Dominic Thorne. Now wouldn't that be ironic, twins in love with the same man! She certainly couldn't allow that to happen.

'Where are you taking me?' she asked sharply, already too confused to delve into what she now felt towards Dominic Thorne. If she felt anything at all!

He shrugged. 'I was just driving around. Until you calmed down.'

'I'm calm now. And I'd like to go home.'

He turned the car in the direction of her home. 'Michael's going to want to see you again—you know that, don't you?'

Her mouth set stubbornly. 'Then he can wait—for ever.'

'Sara——'

'I'm grateful for your support, Mr Thorne, but that's all I am. I won't be seeing Michael Lindlay again.'

'And Marie?' he asked hardly.

She swallowed hard. 'Marie is—well, that's different. I—I said I would call her, and I will.'

'Thank you,' he said softly.

Her aunt was out when Sara let herself into the house, so she was able to collect her thoughts together in private. She hadn't asked Dominic in, and he didn't seem to mind her abrupt departure.

She wasn't an orphan after all! She had a father and a sister, a sister she already loved. It would be impossible not to love someone who looked so much like her, and her affection seemed to be returned.

'You're looking pale, love,' her aunt told her when she returned from the shops loaded down with groceries.

Sara helped her put the food away. She had thought long and hard about mentioning her meeting with her father and Marie to her aunt, and she still didn't know what to do about it. Obviously her aunt and uncle must have known about Marie and herself, which also now explained away her aunt's flustered behaviour when she had broken the cup. It hadn't been the smashed cup that had upset her at all, it had been the mention of Marie's name.

'Sara?' Her aunt was frowning at her now.

She blinked, biting her bottom lip. She hadn't made her mind up what to do about her father, and to talk it over with her aunt was not something she felt like doing at the moment. No matter how kind her aunt and uncle had been to her during this visit, they had also helped to deceive her about the past.

'I—er—I have a headache,' she made up.

'Now that's a shame, I think Eddie wanted to take you out tonight.' Her aunt seemed satisfied with her explanation. 'He said he wanted to see you before you leave.'

'But I'm not going for several more days.'

'You know Eddie,' her aunt teased. 'He's become very fond of you.'

And Sara was fond of him too, in a brotherly sort of way, which was why she accepted his invitation. He took her to the pub they had visited on their first evening together, cheering her up in a way that no one else could have done.

'That's better,' he smiled as she laughed at one of his jokes. 'I was beginning to wonder if I would ever get a smile out of you tonight!'

'Sorry,' she said ruefully, realising that this couldn't

be a very pleasant evening for him.

'Aunt Susan said something about a headache when I rang. Do you still have it?' he asked sympathetically.

They were sitting in one of the booths in the lounge bar, having decided not to join in the darts match this evening. Sara felt relaxed with Eddie, her discovery of earlier today not seeming quite so traumatic now she was with him. But the problem of it had only been pushed to the back of her mind. She knew that tomorrow, or even later today, she would have to think about it once again.

She shook her head in answer to his query. 'No, it's gone. And I'm sorry if I've been a dampener on the evening.'

'Upset about leaving, are you?'

'Oh yes,' she didn't hesitate with her answer. 'England seems like—home.' Even more so now! Her life in Florida seemed like a dream, and England now seemed like reality. Which was pretty stupid when she had lived in Florida virtually all her life.

'Are you thinking of staying on?' Eddie asked interestedly.

She shrugged. 'I—I don't think so. I have to go back for a while anyway. But I—I may come back. I'm not sure.'

He put his hand over hers. 'I'd like you to.'

Alarm flared in her deep brown eyes. 'Eddie——'

'In a purely sisterly sense,' he grinned at her.

She smiled. 'Do you always hold your sister's hand in this way?'

'I don't know, I've never had a sister.'

She burst out laughing. Eddie always managed to reduce things to normality, making her panic this afternoon seem stupid. She wasn't the first person to suddenly discover she had a family, after all, and at least she liked Marie. Her feelings towards her father were harder to define. Her mother had brought her up to love his memory, hence the photograph she always carried with her, and yet when presented with the flesh and blood man, a man still alive, she had recoiled from such a relationship.

And she still recoiled from it! Richard was her father and always would be.

Both her aunt and uncle were still up when Eddie brought her home, so she made coffee for all of them. Eddie seemed to find their determination not to leave them alone very amusing, and finally got up to take his leave.

'They're getting worse than parents,' he joked at the front door.

'Don't say that,' Sara grimaced. 'I've had my fill of parents today.'

'Really?'

'Forget I said that, Eddie,' she advised hastily, realising she was revealing too much. No one must know about Marie and her father until she was ready to accept it herself. 'I've been a bit down the last couple of days. Delayed reaction, I think.'

He gently touched her cheek. 'Never mind, love. Just remember you have Aunt Susan and Uncle Arthur. And there's always me.'

'Thank you.' She gave a quavery smile. 'You don't know how comforting that is. Really!' she insisted at his sceptical look.

'Only I could end up with a beautiful girl like you wanting to be my *friend*,' he said with disgust. 'Or my sister, which is worse,' he grimaced. 'Just my luck!'

Sara reached up and kissed him warmly on the cheek. 'Thank you for being here.'

Eddie frowned. 'When you needed me, hmm?'

'Yes,' she admitted huskily.

' 'Night, love.' He bent to kiss her on the mouth, grinning at her gasp of surprise. 'Brotherly privilege.'

'I'll bet,' she laughed.

Her aunt and uncle were still in the lounge when she returned, and she frowned at their grave expressions.

Something was wrong here, very wrong.

'We had a visitor this evening,' her aunt told her softly, her gaze searching Sara's pale features.

'Oh yes?' They often had visitors, being a very popular couple, so she knew there had to be something special about this particular visitor or else they wouldn't have mentioned it.

'A Mr Dominic Thorne,' her uncle told her, one eyebrow raised questioningly.

Sara drew an angry breath. 'He came here!' she gasped.

Her uncle nodded. 'He seemed concerned about you, wanted to make sure you were all right.'

Her hands clenched into fists at her sides. 'What did he think I was going to do?' she rasped. 'Commit suicide?'

'Now then, Sara,' her uncle chided. 'That isn't the way to be. Susan and I much appreciated his visit.'

'He's told you, hasn't he?' she accused angrily. 'Why couldn't he mind his own damned business?' Her American accent was very strong in her fury.

'He seemed to feel it was his business,' her aunt put in softly.

Her eyes flashed. 'He knew it wasn't—I told him it wasn't.'

'Sara——'

'He had no right to come here,' she stormed, overriding her aunt. 'No right!' she repeated vehemently. 'This is my problem——'

'It was never just your problem,' her aunt told her firmly. 'Both families are involved as well, and Mr Thorne is engaged to your sister.' She shook her head. 'I just couldn't believe it when people started taking you for Marie, not just once but a couple of times. We'd seen photographs of her, of course, the Lindlay family are often in the society columns, but even so we had no idea the similarity was so extreme. Mr Thorne says it's almost impossible to tell you apart.'

Sara's mouth twisted. 'Only almost?' she taunted. 'He seems to have trouble knowing the difference.'

'Really?' Her aunt gave her a sharp look.

'Only my fath—only Michael Lindlay,' she amended quickly, 'could tell the difference. He knew on sight that I wasn't Marie.' She wondered *how* he had known.

'How is Michael?' her uncle asked.

'A bit dazed at the moment,' she revealed huskily. 'I'm afraid I walked out on him this afternoon.'

Her aunt nodded. 'Mr Thorne told us that.'

Sara's mouth tightened. 'What else did he tell you?'

Aunt Susan shrugged. 'Just that you knew about Marie and your father. He thought we should know.'

Dominic Thorne took too much upon himself. She didn't like having her life taken out of her hands in this way. And if he thought he had got away with it then he was in for a surprise!

She sighed. 'I'm not going to ask you for reasons, I'm sure you're as incapable of giving them as Mr Lindlay is.'

'Probably,' her aunt nodded. 'But I can tell you that your mother regretted what happened all her life.'

'I don't believe that! She was happy with Richard, they——'

'Not that part,' Aunt Susan interrupted gently. 'Rachel always regretted taking you away from your sister. I think in the end she would rather have given you up completely than risk the pain you're going through now.'

'No!' Sara cried chokingly. 'No, she loved me. She——'

'Of course she loved you. It was because she loved you, and Marie, that she knew she'd done the wrong thing in separating you. It's strange, really,' her voice broke emotionally, 'but your mother was actually going to tell you about Marie, was going to bring you over here next month on your birthday and introduce the two of you. But fate decided it wouldn't work out that way.'

Sara frowned. 'My mother was really going to do that?'

'Oh yes,' her aunt nodded. 'I can show you the letter if you like.'

'No, no, that won't be necessary. I—I think I'll go to bed now.' She turned blindly out of the room.

'Sara——'

'Leave her, Susan,' she could hear her uncle's firm voice. 'Leave her on her own, she needs time to adjust.'

Time. Everyone seemed to think that with time she would be able to accept this situation. And maybe she would.

She spent a restless night, eating an almost silent breakfast before leaving the house. Her aunt and uncle were still respecting her wish to be left alone, and she felt grateful to them.

The woman behind the desk was the capable middle-aged woman Sara had expected to be Dominic Thorne's secretary.

'Miss Lindlay,' she greeted with a smile. She was a woman of possibly forty-five, her appearance smart, very attractive in a mature sort of way, her ringless hands evidence of her single state. 'Shall I tell Mr Thorne you're here?'

Why not? 'Please do,' Sara's voice was distinctly English.

There was a short conversation on the intercom before the secretary told her to go in.

'Thank you,' Sara smiled.

The inner office was even more impressive, wood-panelled walls, thickly carpeted floor, drinks cabinet and easy chairs, and most impressive of all, Dominic Thorne seated behind the huge mahogany desk.

He looked up as she entered the room, putting down the gold pen he was working with, his smile welcoming. 'Mar——' his eyes narrowed and he frowned. 'But it isn't, is it? Hello, Sara,' he greeted huskily, standing up.

Her irritation was impossible to hide. 'How did you know?' She used her own voice when talking to him.

Dominic shrugged. 'I'm learning, that's all.'

'You mean there is a difference?'

He gave her a considering look, bringing a blush to her cheeks. 'Yes, there's a difference.'

'What is it?' she frowned.

He held back a smile. 'I'm too much of a gentleman to tell you.'

Her eyes flashed. 'You aren't a gentleman at all, which is why I'm here.'

Dominic sighed, moving around the desk to lean back against it. 'I had no idea you wouldn't have told your aunt and uncle everything, the parts they didn't already know anyway.'

'I needed time to think.'

'And have you now thought?' he mocked.

'Not completely.' Sara turned to look at the rows of books in the bookcase along one wall. They were all on engineering, something she knew nothing about.

'What do you need to think about?' he asked from behind her. 'They're your family.'

'Yes,' she agreed dully, turning. 'But it isn't easy accepting that.'

'Why are you here, Sara?' His eyes narrowed. 'Really here, I mean.'

'I told you——'

'The real reason,' he persisted, his blue eyes intent on her pale features.

She flushed, resentful of his perception. 'I came to tell you I didn't appreciate your visit to my aunt and uncle,' she mumbled.

'No,' Dominic shook his head, 'that isn't the real reason, Sara.'

Her head went back in challenge. 'Then what is?'

His face was suddenly harsh. 'Would you like me to tell you—or show you?'

'Sh-show me?' she repeated with a gulp.

His burning gaze on her mouth was almost like a caress, his masculinity at once overwhelming, his sensuality a tangible thing. 'Yes, show you,' he said throatily.

'I—No.' She broke away from the spell he was weaving about her senses, once again looking at the books, but still dangerously aware of him standing a few feet away from her.

'You're right.' He drew in a controlling breath. 'Michael wants to see you.'

'No!' She turned round, and at once wished she hadn't, his gaze burning her at a glance as he seemed to be holding some fierce emotion in check. Sara looked away again, thrown into confusion by—she didn't know by what! She only knew it frightened her, but not in a terrifying way, in a—a *moral* way. This man was engaged to her sister, and yet—and yet——

'Sara!' he groaned achingly.

She swallowed hard. 'I don't want to see Michael Lindlay,' she answered his statement of a few minutes ago, although they had both passed beyond that, and a wild emotion was building up between them, an emotion that threatened to spiral out of control. And that must not be allowed to happen!

Dominic received her silent plea, at once the cool businessman, almost as if Sara had imagined that momentary lapse. But she knew she hadn't imagined it, the wild beating of her heart told her she hadn't.

'He doesn't just want to see you, Sara,' Dominic told her calmly, his raw passion of a moment ago completely erased. 'He wants you to go and live with him, with him and Marie.'

CHAPTER FIVE

'Is he mad?' she cried scornfully.

'No, just a father who wants to get to know his daughter.'

'I surely don't have to go and live with him for that,' she dismissed scathingly.

'It's surely the best way?'

'Not for me! I'm going back to the States in two days' time. I intend resuming my career.'

'You aren't well enough for that.' His voice was sharp. 'Your legs——'

'Are healed.'

'Beautifully,' he nodded. 'As far as it goes. But they aren't strong enough for the arduous job of a model.'

'I'm strong enough to do what I damn well please,' Sara snapped, resenting his bossy behaviour.

'I forbid you—I *ask* you not to do it,' Dominic amended with a shake of his head. 'I'm sorry, I think the last few days have got to me too. You have no need to work, Sara. As Michael's daughter——'

'Will you stop saying that!'

'All right, then,' he bit out angrily, 'as Marie's *sister*, won't you do this?'

Her mouth twisted. 'Because you like to see Marie happy?' she taunted.

'Partly,' he admitted grimly.

'And the other part?'

'For you. I'm sure you can't feel happy about turning your back on your own sister.'

She wasn't. He knew she wasn't. This man knew her, knew everything about her, and it wasn't just because he was close to Marie. 'You aren't being fair,' she choked. 'I don't owe Michael Lindlay anything, least of all loyalty.'

'But you think he owes you something.'

'Yes! No—I don't know,' she said miserably.

'Well, he doesn't. You were happy with your mother, weren't you?'

'Very,' she nodded, frowning.

'Then Michael gave you all he owed you when he let you go. He did, Sara,' Dominic insisted as she went to protest. 'Just think for a moment. Your mother left your father to be with her lover. She shouldn't really have been allowed to take either of her children, and yet Michael let her have you. Why did she never have any other children?' he asked shrewdly.

'Richard wasn't able to have any,' she revealed slowly.

He raised his eyebrows. 'Then Michael did her more of a favour than she first realised. I would have been less charitable.'

'Charitable!' she echoed furiously. 'When he'd been having an affair himself?'

Dominic sighed. 'I can see there's no reasoning with you.'

'None at all,' she confirmed. 'I——'

'Dominic.' For the second time in two days Michael Lindlay walked unannounced into the room containing Dominic and Sara. He came up with a start. 'Sara!' he gasped.

He had aged overnight, even she could see that; there was a drawn look to his handsome face, a bleak look in his eyes. His expression was agonised as he looked at her, seemingly undecided about whether to enter the room or simply leave again.

'Come in, Michael,' Dominic made the decision for him. 'Perhaps you can talk some sense into Sara.'

'I don't think so,' she denied tightly, turning away.

A few seconds later she heard the door close. She didn't know whether she was relieved or saddened that her father had so calmly accepted her refusal to speak to him. She had no doubts that Dominic would never accept such a decision himself. Maybe that was the reason she felt she could rely on him. Even after the way they had reached out to each other just now? She couldn't begin to work out what had happened between them a few minutes ago, except to think that Dominic had momentarily confused her with Marie. That would be the obvious explanation.

'Sara.'

She spun round. Dominic hadn't been the one to remain in the office after all; her father had. She swallowed hard, biting her top lip. 'How is it you were able to tell Marie and myself apart from the start?' she asked shyly.

Some of the tension seemed to leave him, although he still eyed her warily. 'I know my girls,' he said huskily.

She flushed. 'Both of us?'

'Oh yes,' he nodded.

'How?' Her head went back in challenge.

'Photographs of you. And I have Marie with me.'

Sara frowned. 'You have photographs of me?'

He nodded. 'Sent to me by your mother. With Richard's consent, of course.'

'You've corresponded with my mother?' she gasped.

'Occasionally,' he nodded again. 'Although perhaps corresponded is too strong a word. Once a year, sometimes twice, your mother would send me a photograph of you, and I would do the same thing with Marie. I doubt we've written more than a dozen words to each other in twenty years, but the photographs became a ritual.'

'So you've known exactly how I looked all the time?' Sara was having some trouble taking all this in.

He smiled. 'Every step of the way.'

'Did you know that this year you weren't to receive a photograph?' her voice was bitter. 'That my mother and I were actually going to visit you here in England?'

'No,' her father looked startled. 'I had no idea.'

'Apparently my mother considered it time Marie and

I were made aware of each other. I think we should have been told a damn sight sooner than this.'

'I realise you're angry, Sara——'

'Angry?' she repeated tautly. 'I'm furious!' Her eyes sparkled with anger. 'Marie might be able to take all this calmly, but I'm afraid I can't.'

Her father gave a rueful smile. 'Marie didn't accept it calmly either—she gave me hell once you'd left yesterday.'

'Good.' Sara felt some of the anger leaving her. 'I like Marie,' she admitted huskily.

'She likes you too.' There was a shimmer of tears in his deep brown eyes so like her own. 'But not as much as I do. Sara——'

'How about inviting me back for lunch?' she broke in on what she felt could only be an emotional speech. And until she had decided what the future held for her she wanted to keep emotion out of this situation for as long as possible. Even her own anger and resentment must be dampened down for the moment.

'You mean that?' he asked eagerly.

'Why not?' she gave a casual shrug. 'Although I'll have to let my aunt and uncle know where I am.'

'Susan and Arthur? We can call in there on the drive back if you like.'

'I'm not sure——'

'We've remained on quite good terms, if that's what you're concerned about,' her father cut in.

'It seems to have been palsy-walsy all round,' Sara said bitterly.

'I——'

'I'm sorry,' her movements were jerky as she picked up her handbag from the desk-top, 'shall we go now?'

'I just have some papers to collect from my office first. Would you like to come with me or wait here?'

'I'll wait here. You won't be long, will you?'

'Two minutes,' he promised, his eagerness almost embarrassing.

Dominic returned to his office a few seconds later, obviously having been waiting outside. 'There goes a happy man,' he drawled.

'It's only lunch,' Sara snapped awkwardly.

He shook his head. 'Not to Michael it isn't.'

Her eyes flashed at his taunting tone. 'You don't sound as if you approve.'

'Oh, I approve, for Michael's sake.'

'And Marie's!'

'Yes,' the word came out as a hiss. 'But not for my own. And you know why, don't you?' he added harshly.

'No . . .' The awareness was back, only stronger, and once again it frightened her.

Dominic slowly closed the door behind him, his gaze locked on her parted lips. 'Yes, Sara. God, yes . . .!' he groaned, pulling her into his arms. 'I've been wanting this since—since—Oh, God!' His lips ground down on hers.

There was no thought of denial, her mouth opened to accept the probing intimacy of his, her body arched against him. She had never been kissed so intimately, so thoroughly, each touch of Dominic's lips was more drugging than the last.

The situation was spiralling out of control, Dominic's hands probing the curve of her back, sending shivers of delight down her spine, his mouth now caressing the hollow below her ear.

But she was a substitute, Marie's double. It wasn't her he was kissing at all. This realisation made her spin away from him, the fierce desire in his face reaching out hungrily to her, their breathing ragged.

'I have to go,' she said jerkily. 'I—I'll wait for my father outside.'

Dominic made no move to touch her, standing pale and dazed as she quietly left the room.

Sara smiled nervously at the secretary, pushing her long hair back from her pale face. What had happened in there? It had been like a minor explosion, their bodies fusing together in a tide of sensual abandon. Dominic, a man she had believed to be in control at all times, had definitely been out of control for a few brief minutes, had wanted her with every fibre of his body. And she had wanted him too.

But she hadn't been Sara Hamille to him, she had been Marie Lindlay! He seemed to have trouble separating them, and until he could she would have to stay out of his way. If only she weren't so attracted to him!

'Sara!' Her father appeared at her side, a briefcase in his hand. 'Sorry I was longer than anticipated. I just called Marie to make sure she would be at home.'

After what had just taken place between herself and Dominic Sara wasn't sure she would even be able to face Marie.

Luckily she had to visit her aunt and uncle first, which helped to banish Dominic from her mind somewhat. It seemed her father was right about there being no resentment, because Aunt Susan and Uncle Arthur greeted him politely enough.

'Now that we're here I think I'll change, if you don't mind,' she spoke to her father.

'Go ahead.' He seemed quite at ease. 'I'm sure Susan and Arthur will keep me company in your absence.'

Sara hurried to her room, changing from the denims and tee-shirt she had hastily donned that morning and putting on a silky summer dress with a halter neckline and shaped in at the waist. Its tan colour suited her golden skin, making her look cool and composed. At least now she looked more in keeping with a guest of Michael Lindlay.

She hurried downstairs, intending to rescue her aunt and uncle from what could only be an embarrassing meeting, even though they appeared to be putting a brave face on it.

'Sara doesn't know about this, does she?' she heard her aunt say, halting her entrance at these puzzling words. What else didn't she know?

Michael Lindlay sighed. 'It isn't something I find easy to tell anyone, but especially Sara.'

'It's unbelievable,' her uncle said emotionally. 'Poor Sara, I don't think she'll be able to take it. First her mother and stepfather, and now——'

'Ssh, Arthur!' his wife told him. 'I think I heard Sara.'

Sara sighed her frustration. What had her uncle been about to say? First her mother and stepfather, and now——? Now was her *father* going to die too? Oh God, surely not! But what other explanation could there be?

She forced a bright smile to her lips as she breezily entered the room. 'I'm ready,' she announced generally, looking at her father with new eyes. If he was dying, and there could surely be no other explanation, then of what was he dying? He was only in his forties, what could strike a man dead at that young age? A weak heart, a terminal disease? The list was endless. And it made her continued resentment of him seem childish and cruel.

Her father stood up. 'And looking very nice too.' He turned to her aunt and uncle. 'Can I persuade you to join us?'

'Perhaps another time,' her aunt refused.

Sara studied her father on the drive to his home. He didn't look ill, a little strained perhaps, but not ill. Still, some illnesses were like that, the person looking completely normal until it was too late.

Unless she had it all wrong. But what else could have been meant by that conversation?

'Sara!' Marie ran out of the house to greet her as soon as the car drew up outside. She pulled Sara's car door open, tugging her out on to the gravel driveway. 'I couldn't believe it when Daddy rang to say you were coming to lunch.' She hugged her tight. 'After yesterday I didn't think you would ever want to see us again.'

Sara gave a tearful smile. Marie's pleasure was completely genuine. 'Not want to see my own sister?' she choked.

'Oh, Sara!' Marie hugged her all the tighter. 'Isn't it fantastic?' She put her arm through the crook of Sara's. 'We're going to have such fun together,' she told her, taking her into the house.

'Hmm-hmm?'

They both turned at the rather pointed cough. Marie grinned at her father's pained expression. 'Okay, Daddy, you can come too,' she permitted graciously.

'You're so kind,' he grimaced, a lithe, attractive man who didn't look old enough to have twenty-year-old daughters.

Lunch was a lighthearted affair, with Marie and her father doing their best to make Sara feel at home. And to a certain degree they succeeded, all of them greatly enjoying the staff's amazement at there seemingly being two Maries. It took a bit of explaining, but everyone was very welcoming once they knew who Sara was.

'I have to go back to work this afternoon,' their father said regretfully. 'Will you be here when I get back?' He looked hopefully at Sara.

'Well, I——'

'Oh, do stay, Sara,' Marie cut in on her refusal. 'Then after dinner we can——'

'Dinner?' she laughed. 'I only came over for lunch.'

'I want you to stay,' her father told her huskily.

She shrugged. 'All right—dinner.'

He shook his head. 'Not just to dinner, Sara. I want— we *both* want, Marie and I,' he seemed to be having trouble articulating. 'We want you to stay here with us.'

Sara bit her lip. 'Dominic said something about that. I have to go home——'

'This could be your home,' her father cut in. 'With Marie and me.'

'Surely Marie will be getting married soon?' Her voice was shrill at the thought of Dominic marrying Marie. She might have only been a replacement for Marie this

morning, but as far as she was concerned Dominic had
been Dominic, the man she and Marie both loved. Yes,
loved. She had fallen in love with a man who wasn't just
engaged to any woman, he was going to marry her own
sister, a girl she couldn't possibly dislike or fight.

'All the more reason for you to come and live with
Daddy,' Marie said smilingly. 'Then he won't be lonely
when I've gone.'

There was no bitchiness intended in that remark,
Marie just didn't have it in her, and yet Sara realised
that once again she was being used as a replacement.
She had never felt second-best in her life before, but she
did so now. Marie was a lovely, friendly girl, well liked
by everyone, and Sara felt that she was being compared
to her and found wanting. Marie was placid where she
was fiery-tempered, accepted without demur the wishes
of the people around her, namely their father and
Dominic, whereas she rebelled at restrictions being put
on her. Her independent upbringing was possibly responsible for that.

'I want you to come and live with us for yourself.'
Her father perhaps sensed her bitterness. 'After all this
time I would just like us all to be together.'

'I—I'll think about it,' she told him jerkily.

'You go back to work, Daddy,' Marie cut in on the tension. 'Sara and I will go for a swim this afternoon, and I
promise you she'll still be here when you get home tonight.'

'Okay.' He bent to kiss her on the cheek. 'I think
your persuasive powers are a lot stronger than mine.'
He hesitated in front of Sara. 'May I?' he asked huskily.

She raised her cheek in acceptance, watching as he
left the room with long strides. He was a man any girl
would be proud to have as a father, and she was fast
coming round to thinking that way. After all, what had
happened twenty years ago had been a joint decision,
and she had loved her mother very much, so why
shouldn't she eventually come to love her father!
Eventually? The way he had been talking earlier to her

aunt and uncle, there might not be time for 'eventually'.

'Poor Daddy,' Marie giggled. 'All this has put him in a terrible state. He hasn't rested since he found out.'

Sara frowned. 'I don't understand how you can accept it all so easily.'

Marie shrugged. 'Life is too short to make an issue out of something like this. Oh, I know you think Daddy treated you badly, but your mother—*our* mother, treated me just as badly, and I don't resent her. After all, she did leave me behind. New angle?' she quirked a teasing eyebrow.

Sara laughed, nodding. 'New angle.'

Her sister became serious. 'What was she like? Was she beautiful? I mean, we must have got our looks from someone.'

'Conceited!' Sara's eyes twinkled merrily.

'Well, I have to be something to have captured Dominic. Everyone thought he was a confirmed bachelor before he asked me to marry him. I would have been a fool to refuse. Don't you think he's just gorgeous?'

Sara was puzzled. If Marie thought he was so wonderful, and she obviously did, then why did she go out with other men, men Dominic knew about, even though it angered him? Marie didn't seem the sort to try and deceive Dominic, she seemed to love him very much, and yet she had these other men. And she didn't know Marie well enough yet to ask her why she did!

'Sara?' Marie prompted at her continued silence.

'He's very nice.' Her manner was rather stilted, her love for the man a feeling she had never before experienced. 'You'll have to excuse me if I'm a bit reserved about him,' she gave a nervy smile. 'After all, the first time I met him he verbally attacked me, the second time he accused me of all kinds of things.'

'Oh yes,' Marie giggled, 'I can sympathise. You should have heard what he said to me the next day! He's so protective. I think he must be the best friend I ever had. Shall we go for a swim?' she suggested. 'You can wear one of my bikinis, it's sure to fit you. You still haven't told me what our mother was like. Oh dear,' she gave a rueful smile, 'I'm chattering again! Dan— Dominic always says I talk nonsense. And I suppose I do. But I do hate silence, don't you? I never like to be alone,' she grimaced. 'I really hate that.'

Sara was aware that her sister was now chattering not for the sake of it but to cover something up. She hadn't been going to say Dominic at all, she had mentioned someone called Dan and then tried to act as if she hadn't. Who was Dan?

There were so many questions unanswered about the family she now had. Dominic was just as much of a mystery. Why kiss her when he was engaged to Marie?

She mentally shook her head. Each and every one of these people was a complex personality, and she certainly wouldn't be able to analyse them on a few days' acquaintance.

'Our mother was very beautiful, very intelligent. She had a bubbly personality, loved to entertain, and she was very happy with Richard, my stepfather.' Sara shrugged. 'I liked her. And I'm not just saying that because she was my mother.'

'I'm sure you aren't,' Marie agreed readily. 'It isn't always possible to like a parent, even though you love them. I like Daddy too. I think you will when you get to know him better. He really wants you to stay, Sara,' she added wistfully. 'We all do.'

Dominic didn't. He wanted her to go back to the States, and she wasn't sure that wasn't the right thing to do. Wouldn't she just be bringing heartache to herself to stay here, tormenting herself with what she couldn't have?

'I've said I'll think about it,' she told Marie firmly, 'and that's what I'm going to do.'

'Without any pressure from me,' Marie said ruefully. 'Okay, let's go and have that swim.'

The pool was deliciously cool in the heat of the day, situated at the far end of the acre or so of land that surrounded the house, shielded from the house by a high hedgerow. As Marie had thought, her bikini fitted Sara perfectly, its scantiness only just decent.

Sara telephoned her aunt later in the day, and they encouraged her to stay to dinner, saying they had no plans for the evening anyway.

'I think maybe I'm a bit underdressed for dinner.' She looked down at her halter-necked dress.

'You look lovely,' Marie assured her. She frowned. 'Or is that being conceited too?' She shrugged. 'Oh well, it can't be helped—you do look nice. But if you want to wear something of mine then you're quite welcome.'

Sara pulled a face. 'I'm beginning to feel like Little Orphan Annie!'

'How can you be Little Orphan Annie when I'm sure you have lots of clothes at home?' Marie dismissed that idea. 'It must be fun being a model.'

'Hard work,' Sara corrected.

'Mm, I suppose so. I bet if Mummy and Daddy had stuck together I would have been allowed to work too.' Marie flung open the doors to her wardrobe that took up one wall of the bedroom. 'Take your pick,' she invited.

Sara had never seen one person own so many clothes before, and all of them beautiful, the fashion designers' labels showing how expensive they were. She shook her head. 'I'd be afraid of spilling something on them.'

'Don't be silly,' her sister tutted. 'They're only dresses.'

Sara finally allowed herself to be persuaded into wearing a blue velvet dress, the material sensuous against her bare skin. It too was halter-necked, although it revealed a larger expanse of her breasts, and was long and straight to the floor in style.

When Dominic arrived with their father she wished she had turned down this dinner invitation. She hadn't been expecting him, and colour flooded her cheeks as she vividly remembered being in his arms earlier, being kissed by him. She wrenched her gaze away as it seemed to lock with his, glad that she had seconds later as she heard Marie greeting him.

'Darling,' she said softly, the next few moments of silence telling their own story, a painful one to Sara.

She looked up just in time to see Marie moving out of Dominic's arms, her lipstick slightly smudged.

'Sara,' Dominic greeted her abruptly.

'Mr Thorne,' she nodded just as abruptly.

'You can't call my fiancé Mr Thorne,' Marie dismissed with a laugh, her hand resting in the crook of his arm. 'Can she, darling?'

'No,' he agreed curtly.

Sara tried not to call him anything through dinner, concentrating most of her conversation on her father. He was intelligent, amusing, and altogether a charming companion. She was coming to like both members of her family, but falling in love with Dominic made it impossible for her to stay in England.

'Sara?'

She looked up to find her father looking at her enquiringly. 'Sorry?' she blinked her puzzlement.

He laughed. 'It's all right, it wasn't anything important anyway. Did I remember to tell you how beautiful you look this evening? I like the dress.'

She laughed. 'You should—you paid for it!'

He looked startled. 'I did?'

'It's one of mine, Daddy,' Marie grinned. 'Although it never looked that good on me, it must be all that training to be a model.'

Sara blushed at the compliment, studiously avoiding Dominic's piercing blue eyes. He was watching her, she knew he was; he always seemed to be watching her. She just wished she knew why.

'I—er—I think I should be going now,' she suggested brightly.

'I'll drive you,' Dominic offered instantly, almost as if he had been waiting for just such a suggestion.

'No,' she refused sharply, not trusting herself to be alone with this man. 'What I mean,' she added hastily, 'is that I can get a cab—taxi. There's no need to take Dom—Dominic away from Marie this early.'

'You won't be taking me away early,' he drawled. 'I can easily come back.'

'Yes . . .' Sara bit her lip. If he came back he would no doubt spend time giving Marie a prolonged goodbye. Jealousy ripped through her as a physical pain. And then she cursed herself for being a fool. Marie and Dominic could even be sleeping together for all she knew, it was very common in this day and age, and the idea of that was even more unpalatable to her. She couldn't let Dominic drive her home knowing he would be coming back to Marie. 'But I really would rather get a taxi, there's no point in breaking up everyone's evening.'

'You won't be doing that,' Dominic assured her smoothly, standing up to look down at her expectantly.

'Aren't you coming with us, Marie?' she asked her sister almost desperately. 'For the ride?'

'I don't think so.' Marie shook her head regretfully. 'You see, when I've had one of my migraines I usually go to bed early for a few nights.' She grimaced. 'Doctor's orders. I wouldn't do it otherwise.'

'We know that,' her father teased. 'Actually, it's after ten now, so perhaps you ought to go to bed as soon as Sara and Dominic leave.'

Sara and Dominic. Sara repressed the shiver of pleasure that she felt at hearing her name coupled with Dominic's. 'I'd really rather get a taxi, especially as Dominic wouldn't be coming back here.'

Dominic shrugged. 'I have to leave now anyway, so if you want a lift I have an empty car.'

'Of course she'd like a lift,' her father smiled. 'Sara was just being tactful, wanted to leave you two alone.'

'Oh, you don't need to do that,' Marie dismissed. 'I'll just take Dominic outside now and then you won't need to feel in the least guilty. Come along, darling,' and she took her fiancé's hand and led him out of the room.

'You mustn't mind Marie,' her father excused as the door closed after them. 'She's very forthright.'

'Yes.' Sara's cheeks were fiery red as her imagination played overtime. 'I—I like that. My mother——' she broke off, biting her lip.

'Yes?' he prompted. 'Don't stop talking about her because it's me,' he said huskily. 'It's been so long since I heard news of Rachel that I would love to hear about your life with her.'

'I'm sorry,' she said with genuine compassion, realising Dominic had been right about her father's love for her mother. 'My mother brought me up to be completely honest too,' she finished her previous statement.

'We always did have similar views on bringing up children,' he nodded. 'I don't think either of us did a bad job of it.'

At that moment Marie and Dominic rejoined them, Marie's mouth pointedly bare of lipstick. Sara winced, turning away, making her expression blank as she sensed Dominic's gaze on her once again. Marie looked thoroughly, glowingly kissed, and Dominic was looking at *her*.

Why? Did he expect her to act jealous? Was he one of those men who liked to have more than one woman interested in him? Most of all, did he like having *twins* interested in him?

'The dress!' she suddenly exclaimed as they were leaving. 'I still have your dress on, Marie.'

'Well, that's all right,' her sister giggled. 'I'm sure I'll see you again soon.'

'Oh yes, yes, of course.' She gave a jerky smile.

The silence in the car was uncomfortable, Sara not knowing what to say to Dominic now that they were alone.

'You didn't——'

'I hope I——' Both of them began talking at the same time, both of them breaking off at the same time. Sara gave a nervous laugh. 'Go ahead,' she invited.

'It wasn't important,' he dismissed.

She sighed. 'Neither was what I had to say.'

'You don't like being with me, do you?' he guessed bluntly.

'Not much,' she answered with the honesty she had told her father her mother had instilled in her.

'Because I kissed you?'

She blushed in the darkness. 'No,' she answered tautly.

'Liar!' his voice was harsh.

'No lie,' she shook her head. 'You weren't kissing *me*, you were kissing Marie.'

Dominic's laugh was bitter. 'If I kissed Marie like that I'd frighten the hell out of her! I was kissing *you*, Sara. Fool that I am.'

Now he had thrown her into even more confusion. Could her surmise be correct, was he a man who liked more than one string to his bow? And yet he seemed to love Marie very much. Maybe he did love her, but that certainly didn't prevent him being attracted to someone else!

'Then I would appreciate it if you didn't do it again,' she told him tightly.

'I'm trying, Sara,' he revealed grimly. 'I really am trying.'

'Then try a little harder. It's bad enough for me here without having to fight off passes from my sister's boyfriend!'

Dominic's mouth tightened with suppressed anger. And she wasn't surprised. It must be years since anyone had called him a 'boy'. He was thirty-five, all man, and no one could mistake him for anything else. But Sara knew that her only weapon was verbal attack, she was powerless against him physically.

'It wasn't a pass,' he rasped. 'I—I couldn't stop myself.' He obviously hated admitting the weakness. 'But if you'll stay in England I promise it won't happen again.'

'If I go back home it won't happen again either!'

He gave her a sideways glance. 'I could always follow you.'

Sara gasped. 'That wouldn't be very practical,' she scorned.

'For once in my life I would like to act *un*practical!' He was gripping the steering-wheel so tightly his knuckles showed white.

'When *is* the wedding?' Sara asked with pointed sarcasm.

Dominic drew a shaky breath. 'No date has been set yet.'

'Then perhaps it should be. Maybe if you had a wife to keep you busy you wouldn't chase other women.' Her eyes sparkled angrily. 'Marie would be very distressed if she knew about the way you've been acting with me. I believe my father would be too.' There was a threat in her voice, and she knew it had gone home.

A white ring of tension appeared about Dominic's mouth. 'I would prefer you not to tell them.'

'I bet you would!' she scorned.

'Not for the reason you're thinking,' he snapped. 'There's something—a reason you don't understand. If you tell them what happened between us then you'll be causing more damage than you realise. And Marie, and of course your father, are going to need you in the very near future.'

That feeling of foreboding again! Wasn't Dominic just confirming what she already guessed—her father was dying?

'And what about me?' she asked shrilly. 'Who's going to help me?'

His hand moved to grip hers in the darkness, strong and sure, and wholly dependable. 'I'll always be around to help you, you can be sure of that.'

She knew that; hadn't he already become the one person in this whole crazy situation that she knew she could rely on? And yet he was the one she feared the most emotionally, the man who could destroy her at a glance.

'I know,' Dominic said suddenly, huskily, seeming to read her tortuous thoughts. 'And it isn't going to be easy for me either.' He sighed. 'But I swear to you that from now on I'll just be your friend. Stay, Sara,' he pleaded softly. 'Stay, and I'll take care of you.'

She looked up to meet the dazzling passion in his eyes, knowing that she couldn't go back to Florida now even if she wanted to. The man she loved was here, and she had to be where he was.

She nodded. 'I'll stay,' she agreed in a choked voice.

The tension left him in a sigh, and he lifted her hand up to his mouth, kissing the palm with intimate intensity. 'Thank you, Sara! You'll never regret your decision.'

Strange, she already regretted it!

CHAPTER SIX

MARIE was overjoyed by her decision, when she turned up at their aunt and uncle's house halfway through the next morning.

'But how did you know?' Sara frowned, hardly awake yet, having spent a very restless night.

'Dominic rang me this morning,' Marie grinned. 'He rings me every morning.'

Ever the doting fiancé! If it wasn't for the remembered delight of his lips on hers, and the way she quivered with pleasure every time he looked at her, she might have been convinced of his singleminded devotion to Marie. But her own memories were too strong for her to accept that, although she in no way doubted his love for her sister. If only she didn't love him too!

'He said you've decided to stay,' Marie continued excitedly.

After a little 'friendly' persuasion from him! He had half seduced her into making that decision, and she resented him for it.

'I have,' she confirmed. 'But——'

'Move in today!' Marie interrupted eagerly. 'Now! Let's give Daddy a surprise when he comes home.'

Sara looked at her aunt for help. There had been a tearful meeting between aunt and niece, and now Aunt Susan was watching them both indulgently from her usual chair by the window, her knitting in her hand. 'Aunt Susan?' she prompted desperately.

Her aunt shrugged. 'It seems like a good idea to me.'

'But——'

'Your place is with your father and Marie now,' her aunt said firmly.

Of course, her aunt knew of her father's illness. And

of course, she was right, her place was with them. 'It doesn't seem very polite to just walk out on you and Uncle Arthur in this way.' Still she hesitated about committing herself. Staying in the country was one thing, staying where she would have to constantly see Dominic was another.

'Your uncle and I don't mind in the least,' her aunt dismissed that problem. 'You can always come over and visit us. And we would be happier knowing you're still in England, rather than letting you go back to Florida alone.'

Sara could see the sense of that, and knew herself beaten. 'Okay,' she gave in. 'Although I think you should let your—our father know I'm going to be there. I don't want to give him a shock.' Especially as she had no idea what was actually wrong with him.

'Daddy won't be shocked,' her sister assured her. 'He'll be delighted.'

'Maybe Dominic will have told him.'

Marie grinned. 'I asked him not to. Dominic knows how I love to play tricks on people. I used to do it to him all the time. We practically grew up together.'

'He seems a nice man,' Aunt Susan remarked absently.

'Oh, he is,' Marie agreed. 'A bit intense, but very nice. Listen to me!' she giggled. 'Of course I think he's nice, I'm going to marry him. Do you like him, Sara?'

Sara hated the evasion she knew must be in her expression, but she could do nothing about it. 'Yes, I like him. Now, shall we get my things together?' she asked briskly. 'I don't have much, so it shouldn't take long to pack.'

Marie seemed to have enthusiasm even for such mundane tasks as packing suitcases. 'Daddy's going to be so pleased,' she said as she stowed Sara's suitcase in the back of her red sports car, having already taken their leave of Aunt Susan, Sara having promised to visit as often as she could. She had a feeling she was going to need her aunt and uncle's down-to-earth attitude every now and again.

'I hope you're right.' She got in beside her sister.

'I am,' Marie said with certainty. 'Hey, we could have a party, introduce you to all our friends.'

Sara shied away from such a suggestion. 'I don't think so, Marie, not for a while anyway. Let me just get used to being with you and—and Dad first.'

'Don't be silly,' her sister dismissed. 'You don't need to get used to us, we're your family. And I want to show you off to all our friends.'

Sara didn't put up any more arguments, it was useless against Marie's determination anyway. Her sister was used to having her own way, and she did it in such a goodnatured way that it was hard to deny her. Even Dominic, a man Sara felt sure could be very ruthless, both in business and his social life, even he gave in to Marie's slightest whim.

Dominic again! Why couldn't she just put him out of her mind, forget about him? Or at least stop thinking of him every minute of the day and night!

Marie showed her into the bedroom next to her own. 'I knew I could persuade you,' she gave a rueful smile, putting Sara's case down on the bed, 'so I had Edith make up your room for you. Do you like it? If you don't you could always have one of the others. There are six other bedrooms besides Daddy's and mine, so you can take your pick.'

Sara was sure that none of them could be more comfortable than this, the furniture white and delicate-looking, the carpet a deep brown, the bedspread gold with a dark brown velvet headboard, restful paintings hanging on the brown and gold flower-print wallpaper, the curtains a brown velvet.

'This will be fine. But are you sure your father——'

'*Our* father,' Marie corrected firmly. 'And he won't mind at all. Just wait until you see how pleased he is!'

Sara was in her room when her father arrived home,

but she had looked out of the window as soon as she heard the car—*cars*. Once again her father hadn't come home alone, there was the familiar blue Rolls-Royce parked behind her father's Mercedes. Dominic was to be here to dinner again this evening! Oh well, she was going to have to get used to him being around all the time.

She heard her father go to his room to change, and decided that this was the best time to make her presence known.

'Hello, darling,' he answered her knock on his door, for the first time confusing her with Marie. Not that she was surprised, he would hardly expect her to be entering his bedroom. 'Did you see Sara today?' he asked eagerly.

Sara felt a lump rise in her throat at the love he already felt for her. 'Yes,' she said huskily.

'I thought she might be here to dinner.' His eyes were shadowed with his unhappiness.

She smiled, holding out her hands to him. 'I am,' she told him softly. 'I'm here to stay,' she added reassuringly.

'Sara?' He shook his head wonderingly.

She bit her bottom lip to stop it quivering. 'Yes.'

She was at once pulled into a bear-hug; her father's body was shaking as he held her to him. When he finally moved back enough to look down at her there was a bright shimmer of tears in his eyes.

'You don't know how happy you've made me,' he choked.

'I think I do.'

He gave a triumphant shout of laughter. 'Yes, I suppose you do.' His arm remained about her shoulders. 'Now, which bedroom are you in?' She told him. 'Next to Marie,' he murmured almost to himself. 'Oh well,' he shrugged, 'it can't be helped.'

Sara frowned. 'If you would rather I slept somewhere else . . .'

'No,' he reassured her. 'No, I didn't mean that. It's just that sometimes Marie—well, she walks in her sleep.'

'Is that all?' she smiled her relief. 'I can cope with that. Mummy used to do it all the time. Oh, I'm sorry! I didn't mean——'

'Talk about your mother all you want, Sara,' he cut in firmly. 'So Rachel didn't grow out of the habit of sleep-walking?'

'No.' She relaxed a little. 'We used to find her wandering about all over the place.'

Her father nodded. 'Marie started doing it about six months ago. The first time it happened she fell down the stairs.'

'Oh no!' The horror in her face was echoed in her voice. 'Was she hurt?' she asked worriedly.

'Just a bump on the head.' He turned away to put on his tie. 'She had a black eye for several days afterwards.'

'I bet that pleased her!'

'It did,' her father agreed ruefully, pulling on his jacket.

Sara suddenly frowned. 'Six months ago, you said,' she repeated slowly.

He nodded. 'About five-thirty one morning. I wondered what on earth was going on when I heard all the noise.' He grimaced. 'You've no idea how much noise a person falling downstairs can make.'

'This is only a guess,' Sara continued slowly, 'but did Marie fall down the stairs some time in December?'

'I'm not sure. It was—Yes! Yes, it would have been December. I remember now, Marie had a bandaged ankle for Christmas.'

Sara frowned. 'Bandaged ankle?'

'Mm, she sprained her ankle as well as bumping her head.'

'And I bruised my head as well as breaking both my legs—on the twentieth of December,' she added pointedly. 'At twelve-thirty at night.'

Her father was suddenly still. 'What are you saying, Sara?'

'Well, six months ago *I* was involved in an accident, so was Marie, and we both received similar injuries. It just seems too much of a coincidence to me.'

'I suppose so. But as you said, it must just be coincidence.'

Sara shook her head. 'I don't think so. You don't remember the exact date of Marie's fall?'

'Not offhand, no.'

'Then I'll ask Marie, she's sure to remember.'

'Remember what?' Marie appeared in the doorway, spectacularly beautiful in a silver dress that flowed about her as she walked. She grimaced as she saw Sara's surprised expression. 'I have to go to a party at Dominic's mother's this evening. It was too late to get out of it.'

They all walked down the stairs together, Sara's purple dress much more subdued than Marie's but no less attractive, clinging revealingly to the slender curves of her body.

'There's no reason why you should,' she told her sister as they entered the lounge together.

She looked up reluctantly at Dominic, seeing the narrowing of his eyes as he looked at them. He looked magnificent, dressed as he had been the first time Sara had seen him, the black evening suit and snowy white shirt impeccable. Not that Dominic needed these trappings to stand out in any company. He was a man apart, a man who commanded and received attention.

'Which one do I kiss?' he drawled mockingly.

'Guess!' Marie smiled impishly.

Dominic pretended to consider them, although Sara knew he had guessed their identity as soon as they entered the room. After those first few occasions Dominic never confused them. And yet he was pretending to now, bringing Sara out in a hot flush, her breathing shallow as she waited for him to decide.

Her heart stopped beating altogether as he seemed to walk in her direction, changing his mind at the last moment and kissing Marie lightly on the mouth.

He turned to look at Sara. 'Did I have you worried?' he taunted.

'Hardly worried, Dominic,' Marie tapped him lightly on the arm. 'No girl would feel *worried* about being kissed by you.'

'If you say so,' he drawled.

'I do. I was just explaining to Sara that this evening with your mother can't be put off.'

'And I was just saying that it isn't necessary,' Sara said hastily.

'But it's your first night here with us,' Marie protested.

Sara shrugged. 'There'll be plenty of other nights.'

'Why don't you change your mind and come to the party, Michael?' Dominic suggested smoothly. 'My mother was very disappointed that you weren't coming. She's already looking forward to meeting Sara.'

Marie pouted. 'But I wanted to give a party and introduce Sara to everyone.'

Her father smiled indulgently. 'You can still have your party, there'll still be plenty of people for Sara to meet. I doubt your mother has invited all of London, has she, Dominic?'

'Not quite,' the other man smiled at him, joining in his teasing of Marie.

'There you are, then,' their father grinned. 'You'll still have hundreds of people to invite, Marie.'

'I don't want to intrude on your evening,' Sara told her sister. 'And I can surely meet your mother some other time, Dominic,' she added stiltedly.

'Then why not tonight?' he asked, his eyes narrowed.

'Because—well, because——'

'She's a little shy.' Her father put his arm about her shoulders. 'Diane will make you very welcome, Sara. And I did originally have an invitation, I turned it down because of my worry over you. But now that you're here with us I think we should all go. I'm sure the party isn't to be a big one, is it, Dominic?'

'About thirty people.'

Thirty people at the moment seemed like the whole world, but she raised no more arguments. She was just embarrassing herself and everyone else. Besides, what was one evening?

'You were going to ask me something earlier, Sara,' Marie reminded her partway through dinner. 'Something you said I was sure to remember.'

She felt a little foolish about her idea now, especially in front of Dominic, feeling sure he would just ridicule her. Dominic was a man who dealt in facts, a man of logic, and what she was suggesting certainly wasn't logical.

She looked down at her succulently cooked chicken, wishing she had an appetite for it. 'I just wondered what the date was when you fell down the stairs,' she shrugged dismissively. 'It isn't important. I'm sure you don't even remember it.'

All humour had left Marie, leaving her face haunted. 'I remember exactly,' she said hollowly. 'It was the twentieth of December.'

Once again Sara's interest flared. 'The same day!' she told her father excitedly. 'Don't you see, it's the same day!' She clutched his arm.

'But a different time,' he shook his head. 'It has to be a coincidence.'

'You've forgotten the time difference, Dad.' She didn't even notice she had called him that in the excitement of this discovery, but the other occupants of the dining-room table did. Her father flushed with pleasure, Marie and Dominic smiled approvingly. 'It was five-thirty here,' she explained, 'but twelve-thirty in Florida.'

'The same day as your accident,' Dominic suddenly realised.

'Yes!' She looked at him, her eyes glowing. Then she frowned. 'But how did you know that?'

'The file,' he reminded her.

'Oh yes,' she nodded absently. 'Don't you think it's weird?'

'Extremely so,' he surprised her by agreeing.

Over the next few minutes they discovered that these similarities had occurred several times during the last twenty years, a case of them both having measles at the same time, both having their tonsils out within days of each other. The list was endless once they started comparing notes, and each new discovery added to their amazement.

'Maybe we'll both fall in love with the same man,' Marie said mischievously, not knowing how near the truth she was, or Sara felt sure she wouldn't have said it. Marie wasn't in the least vindictive or cruel, and the remark would have been both those things if she had known of Sara's feelings. 'How would you like that, darling?' she teased her fiancé.

His expression was grim, his mouth a thin taut line. 'I wouldn't like it at all,' he said curtly.

'I was only joking, Dominic,' Marie was instantly contrite. 'I'm sure Sara already has a boy-friend in America.'

Dominic looked at Sara with sharp eyes. 'Do you?' he demanded abruptly.

She thought of Barry and then dismissed him. 'Not in America, no,' she replied slowly. 'But I have a—friend here. His name is Eddie.' And she hoped Eddie would forgive her for using him in this way. But she needed some form of defence, was afraid to let Dominic know just how deeply she had become interested in him.

'You work fast,' he snapped. 'After all, you've only been here a little under two weeks.'

She gave him a brittle smile. 'Sometimes it takes only a glance to feel you know someone, like them.'

'Love them?' he prompted tautly.

She gave what she hoped was a light laugh. 'It's a little too soon to tell.'

'You'll have to invite Eddie over one evening,' her father suggested. 'I'd like to meet him.'

Sara shrugged. 'Maybe the night of the party.'

'Then we must have the party very soon,' Marie said eagerly. 'How about Saturday?'

'That's a little too soon for me,' Sara refused laughingly. 'Maybe next week, hmm?'

'All right,' her sister accepted reluctantly, looking at her wristwatch. 'I think we should be leaving now.'

At once the nervousness returned to Sara. She didn't want to meet Dominic's mother, to know about his family, his home life. Somehow that would bring her even closer to him, make it all the harder for her to accept his marriage to her sister.

She travelled with her father in his car, Marie and Dominic in the Rolls. At least she had been given this respite, time to collect together the poise and control she had been taught during her career, something that seemed to have deserted her the last few days, along with her carefree nature.

'Relax,' her father seemed to sense her tension. 'I can assure you that Diane is a most gracious hostess.'

'I'm sure she is. It's just—well——'

His hand moved to clasp hers. 'You'll be fine, Marie and I will see to that.'

Diane Thorne's house was just what Sara had expected, a detached house set in its own grounds, a butler to show them in and take their wraps, a maid to show them into the gracious lounge where a dozen or so people were already chatting around the room in groups of twos and threes.

The entrance of Marie and herself caused just as much of a sensation as she had known it would. It had been this attention that she had been dreading, and when she felt her father's arm go protectively about her waist she leant gratefully back against him.

'Come and meet my mother,' Dominic murmured against her earlobe.

Sara turned with a start, quickly moving out of the arc of his arm. 'I didn't realise—I thought you were my father!' she accused.

'I told him I would take care of you—Marie has taken him to get a drink. Now come and meet my mother,' he repeated firmly.

She nodded, licking her lips nervously; Dominic's touch had completely unnerved her.

Dominic put a guiding hand under her elbow. 'I'm sorry about earlier,' he said huskily. 'It was—a stupid thing to do.'

'I'm sorry?' She shook her head, determinedly not looking at him, knowing that people were watching them as they moved across the room. 'I don't know what you mean.'

His hand tightened. 'I was almost tempted to kiss you and not Marie,' he revealed gruffly. 'It was an utterly stupid move on my part. Who is Eddie?' he demanded tautly.

She shrugged. 'A friend—I told you.'

Dominic turned her to face him, his expression fierce. 'How much of a friend?' he wanted to know.

'Really, Dominic!' her tone was deliberately taunting 'My friendship with Eddie is none of your business.'

His eyes turned almost black, his gaze compelling. 'You know damn well it is! Sara——'

'Dominic!' A small woman with grey-black hair appeared at his side, a beautiful woman, her make-up and figure impeccable for her age, which must have been at least fifty. Looking at her closely, Sara could see certain resemblances to Dominic, the same deep blue eyes, the same determined chin, so she guessed this to be his mother, which meant she was well over fifty. The woman turned to Sara, a warm smile to her lips. 'You must be Sara,' she held out her hand.

She blushed, taking that hand. 'It's nice to meet

you, Mrs Thorne,' she said shyly.

The other woman shook her head. 'Your likeness to Marie is incredible!'

Sara smiled. 'And yet you knew the difference.'

Diane Thorne glanced at her son. 'Go and get Sara and me a drink, darling.'

For a moment Dominic looked like ignoring that imperious demand, then with an angry glare at his mother he turned and walked in the direction of the bar.

Both women watched him go, Sara with relief, and his mother with—Sara couldn't tell the other woman's feelings, deliberately so, she felt.

'My father and Marie——'

'Are talking to my other son,' Diane Thorne nodded.

Sara's eyes widened. 'I didn't realise you had another son.'

'And a daughter too. I'll introduce you to them both later, and to Samantha's husband Brett. They're expecting their first child soon, my first grandchild.' She smiled. 'I'm not sure I'll like being a grandmother, it's very ageing,' she grimaced.

Sara laughed at her rueful expression. 'My mother always said you're only as old as you feel.'

'A good saying.' Blue eyes twinkled merrily. 'As long as you don't feel a hundred at the time!'

Sara spluttered with laughter. 'I know that feeling.'

'Dominic tells me you're a model,' Mrs Thorne said interestedly.

She frowned at the mention of Dominic. 'I was. I'm not sure what I am any more,' She shrugged. 'My father doesn't appear to approve of women working for a living.'

'You mean Marie?'

'Mm,' Sara nodded.

Diane Thorne shrugged. 'I'm sure your father will respect your wish for independence. Marie is different, she likes acting as hostess. She's going to make

Dominic a wonderful wife.'

'Yes,' Sara agreed hollowly, watching Dominic as he strode across the room towards them, the requested drinks in his capable hands.

His mother gently touched her arm. 'Don't,' she pleaded huskily.

Sara looked stricken. 'Don't what, Mrs Thorne?'

The other woman's eyes were filled with compassion. 'Don't love my son, Sara.'

'I——'

'Here we are.' Dominic handed his mother her drink, frowning as he looked at Sara's pale face. 'Sara?' he queried sharply. 'Sara, what's wrong?'

'Nothing. Nothing is wrong! I—Excuse me.' She pushed past him, heading for the open doors that led to the moonlit garden. She trembled in the warmth of the evening, wondering how Diane Thorne had guessed her feelings so quickly.

'Sara!' Dominic spun her round to face him, forcing her chin up. 'What did my mother say to you?' he rasped.

'I—Nothing.' She looked down at her feet. 'I—I just felt faint for a moment.' She forced a smile to her numb lips. 'I'm all right now. Shall we go back inside?' She made a move towards the door.

'No!' Dominic stopped her, a fevered look in his eyes. 'I want to know what my mother said.'

'She—she—Oh, what does it matter?' she dismissed impatiently, her gaze locked on the strength of his face, the sensuousness of his firm mouth, and she couldn't break free of the spell he was casting on her. 'Dominic!' she groaned, swaying into his arms.

He needed no further encouragement, but devoured her lips with his own, his arms like steel bands about her. Their hearts beat as one, their desire flamed as one, their mouths joined even if their bodies couldn't be.

'Oh God, Sara,' Dominic moaned into her throat, his mouth sending liquid fire through her veins. 'I want you so damned much!' he agonised, his lips touching the firm curve of her breasts.

She feverishly unbuttoned his shirt, her hands moving inside to caress the hard strength of his back and chest. She had never touched a man this intimately, loving the silky texture of his skin, the ripple of muscles as he quivered beneath her touch. He felt so good, so sensually warm and exciting that Sara just wanted to lose herself against him, and she knew he felt the same way, could feel the throbbing hardness of his thighs, his ragged breathing as her fingertips caressed lower to his waist.

Neither of them had the strength to stop this explosion of emotions between them, their hands roaming freely over each other's bodies, straining for a much closer contact.

'I want to possess you!' Dominic shuddered against her as he fought for control. 'I want to feel you naked against me, to know every inch of your body, every quivering nerve. Am I frightening you?' he groaned as she trembled.

'You're exciting me,' she instantly denied fear. 'I want that too, Dominic. I want you so badly!' She blushed at her own admission.

'When, my darling?' he moaned, caressing her breast through the material of her dress. 'When will you be mine?'

'Whenever you want me,' she told him breathlessly, aiding his entry down the low cleavage of her dress, her breath catching in her throat as his hand closed possessively over her bare breast.

'*Now*,' he groaned. 'I want you now!'

Sara gasped as her nipple hardened and rose to the touch of his fingertips, feeling herself swell into his waiting hand, raw desire ripping through her body. 'Oh God, Dominic!' She swayed against him, almost fainting with her need of him.

'Dominic? Dominic!'

Panic washed over Sara as she realised that was

Dominic's mother calling to him. God, she thought, what must the other woman be thinking; they had been out here ages!

'It's your mother,' she told him in a choked whisper. 'I—She—You have to go in, Dominic.'

If anything his hold tightened about her. 'And leave you here all alone?' He shook his head. 'I can't do that. I never want you to be alone again, Sara. I want to take care of you, but not as a friend, I want you as a——'

'Lover?' she queried shakily. 'It wouldn't do, Dominic. No man could bed two sisters, in all decency.'

He closed his eyes as if to shut out the pain. 'At this moment I don't feel decent. I feel——'

'Dominic!' His mother's call was an angry whisper now. 'Dominic, we have guests!' She was obviously very agitated.

He gave an angry sigh, reluctantly buttoning his shirt. 'I have to go in, Sara. I don't want my mother coming out here.'

Neither did she; her senses were still very much attuned to Dominic's caresses. 'Yes—go. I—I want to stay here for a while. If anyone asks, my father or Marie, tell them I have a headache I'm trying to clear.'

His shaking fingers gently touched her cheek. 'You won't be long?'

'No.' Just long enough to calm down from the excitement he had caused in her body.

'Oh, Sara, I wish—God, I wish——'

'Please go in, Dominic,' she begged shakily. 'Please!'

With great reluctance he turned to go, stopping suddenly to turn and look at her. 'I won't forget about tonight, Sara, so don't ask me to.' His eyes were still alight with his own passion. 'And whatever my mother said to you——'

'She said for the best,' she cut in firmly. 'Now go. But first . . .' she reached up and wiped all traces of her lip-gloss from his mouth.

His answer was to once again bend his head and crush

her lips with his own, this time wiping his mouth himself, not angrily or roughly, but sensuously soft, as if feeling the taste of her lips against his fingertips. With one last telling glance he was gone, and Sara felt her body relax from the tension she had been under.

She was mad, insane, and yet if she were insane then so was Dominic. He had lost all control, didn't seem to care that someone could have walked out here at any moment and caught them in what could be called a compromising situation. But perhaps his mother had made sure that didn't happen, had somehow prevented anyone from coming out here.

Where would it all end? How could such a situation have an *end*? She wanted and loved Dominic, Dominic obviously wanted her, and yet he loved Marie. Sara loved Marie too, could never hurt her in any way, and yet that love didn't seem to matter when confronted with her wild longing for Dominic. How could he want both of them? How could he do that to either of them? At least Marie didn't know he was cheating her, at least she was being spared that pain. But Sara knew all about his duplicity, was in fact the 'other woman' in this affair. Once again she asked herself where it would all end.

She stepped back into the shadows of the garden as someone else came out on to the balcony, still not feeling up to seeing anyone just yet. The shadow of another person approached, and the first person let out a gasp of dismay.

'Go away, Danny!' Marie could be heard saying.

Danny? Sara instantly became alert. The other day Marie had been about to say Dan—something. Could this be the Danny she had been talking about?

'Marie——'

'Leave me alone!' She pushed him away from her. 'You know you shouldn't be out here with me.'

'You knew I'd follow you,' the man protested, his voice strangely familiar to Sara.

But why was it familiar? She didn't know anyone called Danny in England.

'Marie, we have to talk,' he went on. 'This marriage to Nick just isn't on.'

Nick, this man called *Dominic* Nick! She had met only one person who did that, the man she had met in Soho. That must be the reason his voice was so familiar.

'You're wrong, Danny,' Marie told him firmly. 'My marriage to Dominic is very much on. In fact, he's the only man I would marry.'

'Last year you wanted to marry me,' the man reminded fiercely.

'I made a mistake. Every girl is entitled to make one,' Marie said lightly. 'You were mine. But I'm over that now, and I'm going to marry Dominic.'

'I won't let you!' Danny pulled her into his arms. 'I love you, Marie, and you love me.'

Sara was embarrassed at being a witness to this conversation, but it was too late to move now.

Marie emerged from Danny's suffocating kiss. 'Let me go, Danny,' she ordered coldly. 'My sister's out here somewhere. She's the reason I'm out here at all—I came to look for her.'

At the mention of her Sara's foot accidentally knocked against one of the flower-pots standing along the verandah, and she moved back into the shadows.

'I heard someone,' Marie whispered, pushing Danny away from her. 'Please, you have to go. That could be Sara, and I don't want her to see me with you. Please, Danny!' she pleaded as he still didn't move.

'All right!' he accepted angrily. 'But this isn't the end of it. I won't let you marry Nick.'

Even from this distance Sara could see Marie's eyes flash, her chin thrust out in challenge. 'Try and stop me,' she hissed. 'Just try it, Danny. I'll never come back to you. Never!'

'We'll see!' he snapped before turning around and going back into the house.

Sara heard her sister's ragged sigh, giving her a few minutes to collect herself before making her presence known. Even in the gloom she could clearly see Marie's paleness, her wide distressed eyes.

But all this was quickly masked as she saw Sara, her smile on the shaky side. 'How are you feeling now?' she asked concernedly.

'A lot better,' Sara replied, remembering the headache she was supposed to have. 'I—Shall we go back inside?' She wished she could show Marie that she knew of her distress, but without revealing her eavesdropping she couldn't very well do that.

They rejoined their father and Dominic, and Marie was the one who looked ill. Dominic's arm came about her protectively.

'I think it's time we went,' he said softly. 'You're looking tired, Marie.'

'I—I think maybe I am,' she agreed hesitantly. 'It must be the—the heat.'

Or her rather heated meeting with the young man called Danny! Sara was in utter confusion about her newly acquired family. So many secrets, past and present, that she just didn't have access to.

CHAPTER SEVEN

MARIE threw herself wholeheartedly into the preparations for their own party, or perhaps wholeheartedly was the wrong description; mindlessly fitted better. She was like a butterfly, flitting from one arrangement to another, never seeming to stop long enough to think, let alone plan anything.

And then mid-week she fell prone to one of her migraine attacks. Sara heard her moving restlessly about her room in the middle of the night, and at first she stayed awake in case Marie began sleepwalking. Then she realised that the frenzied walking was due to something else. Marie was in pain of some sort, whether physical or mental she didn't know, she only knew her twin was in pain.

Marie was sitting on the bed when she went in, bent double, her head cradled in her hands. 'Oh, God, make it stop,' she groaned. 'Make it stop!'

'Marie!' Sara ran to her, holding her against her shoulder. 'Marie, what is it?'

'My head!' her sister choked. 'Oh, God, make the pains stop!' Tears streamed down her face.

'What sort of pains, Marie?'

'Sharp, *digging* pains,' she quivered. 'I can't stand it, Sara. I just can't stand it!' she repeated hysterically.

'It's all right now, honey,' Sara soothed. 'I'm with you. Now we're going to make the pains go away. You and I together are going to make them stop. Now lie back, Marie. Come on, back on the bed.' All the time she was talking she was easing her sister back on the pillows. 'That's the way,' she crooned once Marie was finally lying down. 'Now I'm going to turn out the light——'

'No! No, don't leave me in the dark!' Marie struggled to sit up again.

'I'm not going to leave you at all,' Sara reassured her, holding her firmly against her. 'I'm going to stay right here with you.'

'Please don't turn off the light,' her sister trembled. 'I don't like the dark. It—it makes me think of death.' She swallowed hard. 'Do you think when you die that it's all darkness, that you're alone in the dark for ever?'

Sara frowned, smoothing Marie's heated brow, feeling the tension starting to recede. 'I don't think so,' she comforted.

'Don't you really?' Marie asked hopefully.

'I really don't.'

Right now she would give anything to know how long Marie's headaches had been occurring. She would take a bet on its being since she had found out about their father's illness. These migraine attacks were brought on through fear of her father's death. Marie was one of those people petrified of death and all it entailed. It held such a fear for her that she had nightmares, sleepwalked, and had these terrible tension headaches, headaches that caused actual physical pains.

'All right,' Marie sighed against her. 'You can turn out the main light now. But leave on the bedside lamp!' she pleaded.

'I will,' Sara reassured her. 'But I'm sure a dim light will help your head.' She rejoined her sister on the bed, putting her arms about her and holding her tight. 'I'm here now, Marie,' she murmured. 'You can go to sleep, you aren't alone any more.'

'Thank you,' Marie sighed. 'I—I feel better now.' She closed her eyes, starting to relax. 'I'm sorry to be such a baby,' she murmured.

'You aren't a baby,' Sara smoothed her sister's hair. 'You're in pain, and you're naturally upset.'

'The pain's going now.'

Of course it was; Marie had been comforted and reassured, and now the headache was fading. As the pain receded sleep took over, and it wasn't long before Sara knew her sister to be asleep. But still she didn't leave her, feeling that Marie needed her close, could sense she was there even though she was now fast asleep.

Someone ought to be told the reason for Marie's migraine attacks. They were very serious, their father's worried return from his business trip had been evidence of that, and yet they could all be stopped if Marie were able to discuss her father's illness with someone. At the moment she was obviously afraid to, and as Sara wasn't even supposed to know about the illness she couldn't really introduce the subject. The trouble was she didn't yet know her father or sister well enough to interfere in this situation. That left only Dominic.

But she couldn't talk to Dominic either, had avoided even looking at him the last couple of days; the memory of their behaviour out in his mother's garden was still too vivid in her mind for her to think of it without blushing. She had behaved shamelessly, had given in to a passion that she had never known before, a desire to be possessed by Dominic, her own sister's intended husband.

Dominic hadn't accepted her cool behaviour of the last few days without demur, but there was little he could do in front of Marie and her father. Any attempts by him to get her alone she had so far managed to rebuff, and yesterday when she had received a telephone call from a man who wouldn't give his name she had refused to take the call, guessing it to be Dominic. They had to stay away from each other, and if Dominic wasn't strong enough to see that they did then she would have to be the one who did.

Some time towards morning she must have fallen asleep herself, because the sun was filtering through the curtains when next she opened her eyes. A quick look at the bedside clock showed her it was almost eight o'clock. Marie would be all right now, now it was daylight, and

as she was still asleep, Sara moved gingerly from her
side and made her way back to her own room.

She met her father out in the corridor, his dark pinstriped suit evidence of his having just prepared to go to
work.

He frowned as he saw her softly close Marie's bedroom door. 'Has she been ill?' he asked worriedly.

'Just one of her headaches,' Sara shrugged. 'I think
she's all right now.'

'I'll go in to her.' His hand moved out to the door-
handle.

'No,' Sara stopped him. 'She's asleep. I should leave
her.'

He looked taken aback. 'She actually managed to fall
asleep? Usually when she has one of these attacks
someone has to sit up with her all night.'

This made Sara wonder how many times Dominic
had been the one to sit through the night with Marie.
After all, their father had been out of the country when
she had had her last attack.

She pushed these thoughts to the back of her mind,
knowing that Dominic's relationship with Marie, the
closeness of it, was none of her business. 'She's asleep
this time!' Her voice was sharper than she intended with
the intimacy of her thoughts.

'What did you do?' Her father was still obviously
amazed by this unusual occurrence.

'Sat with her, talked with her. Then I just held her
while she went to sleep. She doesn't like the dark,' Sara
added tautly, wishing she could tell him *why* she didn't.

He looked away. 'I know,' he admitted grimly.

'I think Marie should see a doctor,' she insisted firmly.
Maybe if Marie could tell her fears to a doctor he could
pass them on to their father.

'She's seen one, more than one.'

'And?' Sara prompted.

'Just tension headaches,' he dismissed with a shrug.
'Probably due to her engagement to Dominic and the

excitement of getting married. They tell me a lot of engaged girls get them.'

'That bad?' she scorned.

'Sometimes,' he nodded, and glanced down at his wrist-watch. 'I have to go down now, I just have time for breakfast before my early appointment.' He bent to give her a preoccupied kiss on the forehead. 'I'll see you later, darling. I should leave Marie, she usually sleeps all day after one of these attacks.'

'I doubt she will today, not when she's slept most of the night.'

'Maybe not. I should get some rest yourself, Sara. It must have been a long night for you.'

Sleep was out of the question now, now that she had thought of Dominic. 'I think I would rather dress and have breakfast,' she smiled at her father.

He nodded. 'Then I'll wait downstairs for you.'

It didn't take her long to shower and dress in her usual denims and casual top, this time a short-sleeved checked shirt, the top two buttons left undone for coolness. She checked on Marie before she went downstairs, and found her sister still fast asleep.

She joined her father at the breakfast table, pouring them both out a cup of coffee. 'These migraines of Marie's,' she persisted, 'does she always have so many? I mean, it isn't long since the last one.'

'They have become a little more—frequent lately,' her father admitted, 'But I'm sure it's nothing to worry about.'

'When did she last see a doctor?'

'A couple of weeks ago. Please don't worry about it, Sara,' he smiled. 'Marie will be over it by tomorrow.'

She frowned. 'Not today?'

'Not usually.' He looked thoughtful. 'I think she was supposed to be acting as Dominic's hostess this evening too.'

'Surely he can put it off?'

Her father shook his head. 'These clients are only in

town for this evening. Oh well, I'm sure Dominic will think of something.'

He did; he asked Sara to take Marie's place. He arrived shortly before lunch to visit his fiancée, spending some time alone with Marie in her bedroom.

Sara began to tremble as he joined her in the lounge, and put down the book she had been pretending to read since he had arrived, pretending because she certainly couldn't concentrate knowing Dominic was in the house.

'How is she?' she asked for something to say, knowing how Marie was, because she had been in to see her herself only half an hour earlier.

'Fine,' Dominic confirmed her earlier findings. 'How have you been?' he asked huskily.

'Me?' she said brightly. 'Oh, I'm very well. It's Marie I'm worried about. My father doesn't seem all that concerned——'

'Then I'm sure he knows best,' Dominic interrupted.

'Are you?' she derided. 'Aren't you in the least concerned about her either?'

Dominic's mouth tightened, his eyes narrowing. 'What are you implying?' he demanded tautly.

Sara moved impatiently, standing up to pace the room. 'It seems to me that no one takes these attacks of Marie's seriously. It isn't natural——'

His hand came out to grab her arm, his fingers biting painfully into her wrist. 'Don't interfere in things you don't understand. You haven't been here long enough to realise——'

She pulled out of his grasp. 'To realise what?' she asked furiously, her eyes sparkling dangerously. 'That neither my father or you seem to give a damn about Marie, that you even make passes at me behind her back?'

'Passes!' Dominic ground out fiercely, his handsome face alight with anger. 'You think they're *passes*?' he asked incredulously.

Her stance was challenging. 'What else could they be?'

He sighed, his anger fading. 'If you only knew . . .'

'Something else I shouldn't know?' Sara snapped tautly. 'Something else I haven't been in this family long enough to be privileged to hear? Your own words, Dominic,' she scorned at his darkening expression. 'I haven't been here long enough to understand!' she repeated in a choked voice, turning to run out of the room and up the stairs.

She knew that Dominic followed her, could hear the pounding of his feet on the stairs, could hear him panting not far behind her. But she hoped to reach her bedroom and lock the door before Dominic caught up with her, knowing he would never dare cause a scene outside her bedroom door, not with Marie so close.

What she hadn't taken into account was the fact that there was no lock on her door. Dominic crashed into the room after her, closing the door behind him, moving towards her with determined strides.

'No, Dominic!' She cowered back against the far wall.

There was a strange expression in his eyes, a glazed look that showed her he hadn't really heard her protest. 'You made me come up here,' he muttered, 'made me follow you to your bedroom. Sara . . .!'

He loomed over her like a dark shadow, and Sara knew he was right. She *had* made him follow her, whether intentionally or subconsciously she didn't know. But he was here now, and the outcome of this was as inevitable as the setting of the sun.

She moved forward to meet him, their bodies moulding together like two parts of a broken sculpture. Sara felt truly at home for the first time in days, knew this was where she belonged, where she wanted to be. But with her sister in the next room——!'

Dominic seemed to sense her withdrawal and let her go with great reluctance, a rueful expression on his face as he looked down at her. 'I just can't keep my hands off you,' he groaned, running his hands through the thickness of his hair. 'But this isn't the place, hmm?'

Her gaze went unwillingly in the direction of Marie's bedroom. 'Nowhere is the right place for us. You've got to leave me alone, Dominic,' she pleaded. 'I can't say no to you——'

'For God's sake never say no!' he agonised, his handsome face flushed with wanting her. 'I need you, Sara. I need your presence here.'

She swallowed hard. 'A few days ago you wanted me to leave England and never come back.'

'You know why.' His gaze was heated. 'And I've been proved right. Every time we meet I——' he broke off, biting his lip. 'My mother liked you.'

'Did she?' Sara blushed, knowing what had sparked that comment. His mother must have guessed what had been happening out in the garden, especially after guessing how she felt about Dominic.

'Very much,' he nodded. 'She would like to meet you again.'

'She will.' She put a nervous hand up to her hair, thinking what a strange conversation this was to be having in her bedroom. 'At the party, on Saturday,' she reminded him.

Dominic smiled. 'I meant somewhere less public.'

Sara bit into her bottom lip, uncaring of the pain she caused. Physical pain was as nothing compared to the emotional hunger of loving Dominic. 'Dominic . . . Your mother, she—she knows,' she revealed hesitantly.

His eyes narrowed and he stopped his pacing of the room to look at her. 'Knows what?'

She licked her lips, unaware of how provocative she was being, but suddenly noticing Dominic's gaze fixed on her mouth. She blushed fiery red. 'At the party she—she warned me, your mother. She doesn't approve of—of——'

'You?' he asked furiously, his eyes blazing.

In that moment he looked more like the man she had first met, the self-assured arrogant man who wouldn't suffer fools gladly. 'No, not me exactly,' she hastened to assure him, not wishing to bring this anger down on his mother. 'Just this—this situation.'

'It isn't a situation,' he dismissed disgustedly. 'It's a bloody mess!'

Her mouth quirked into a derisive smile. 'Yes,' she agreed shakily. 'Could we go back downstairs?' she suggested nervously. 'I'm not sure how thick these walls are, and Marie—well, she could hear all this.'

'Yes,' he sighed. 'We should go back downstairs. God, it's so good to talk to you again, Sara. I know you've been avoiding me, and I also know the reason for it, but if I promise——'

'No, Dominic!' she warned. 'No more promises.'

His expression was rueful. 'I made a poor job of keeping this last one, didn't I?'

'Yes.'

'Sara——'

'Please, let's go downstairs!' Her voice was shrill.

'Oh yes, yes, of course.'

All the time she was walking down the stairs she was aware of his gaze burning into her back. Normally he seemed such a self-controlled, arrogant person, and yet whenever he was near her this veneer seemed to fall away and he became a passionately demanding man. She had no doubt that he loved Marie, and yet that love was nothing like the consuming fire that flared up between *them* every time they met, a fire that threatened to flame out of control.

'What are you thinking?'

She looked up to find Dominic watching her with narrowed eyes. 'I was just wondering about you and—and Marie.'

He stiffened. 'What about us?'

Sara took her courage in both hands, lifting her head

high to meet his watchful blue eyes unflinchingly. 'Do you sleep with her?'

'No!' the denial exploded out of him.

'There's no need to be so vehement,' she scorned, relief washing over her. 'You seem to want to sleep with me.'

'That's different,' he snapped.

'Really?' she taunted. 'Why is it?'

'Because—well, because—Do you sleep with Eddie?' he attacked in a vicious voice.

'Eddie?' she frowned. 'No, of course not. And talking of Eddie,' she gave a hurried look at her wrist-watch, 'I'm meeting him for lunch. If I don't leave now I shall be late.'

'Sara!' Dominic's call stopped her at the door. 'Don't go,' he requested huskily.

'I have to.'

'Why?' he groaned.

'Because I never let my friends down.'

'Do I count as a friend?'

'Hardly!' she derided.

'How about Marie?' he asked softly.

Sara flinched. 'You bastard!' she glared at him. 'You almost attack me every time we meet, and you have the nerve to remind *me* of my loyalty to Marie!'

He closed his eyes. 'I wasn't doing that, I was just asking you if you would let Marie down.'

'I already have,' she said bitterly, 'and I'm not proud of the fact.'

'Neither am I!'

'You could have fooled me!'

His mouth tightened into an angry line. 'You either infuriate me or inflame me, and at the moment I can't cope with either emotion.'

'What do you think you do to me?' she groaned. 'Oh God, I can't stand any more of this—I'm going out!'

'Marie wants you to stand in for her tonight,' Dominic revealed in a rush.

Sara frowned. 'At your dinner party?'

'How did you know about that?'

'My father mentioned it.'

'I see. Yes, that's it. Marie wondered whether you could take her place?' He eyed her questioningly.

'At the table, or in your bed?'

'Please, Sara,' he groaned, 'don't!'

'That's what your mother said,' she remembered bitterly.

Dominic frowned. 'Don't what?'

She shrugged. 'Don't become involved with you.' She couldn't reveal that his mother had guessed at her love for him!

'Are you involved?'

'You're going to marry my sister,' she stated the obvious involvement.

'Yes,' he sighed heavily. 'Will you act as my hostess tonight?'

'Why can't your mother do it? You live with her, don't you?'

'Hardly,' he gave a half smile. 'None of us live with her, we all fled the nest long ago. I have a penthouse apartment in town.'

Her eyes widened. 'And that's where I would be expected to act as your hostess?'

'Yes.'

Sara shook her head in alarm. 'I can't. You know I can't!' she groaned.

He made no move to touch her, and yet his eyes caressed wherever they looked. 'It would make Marie happy,' he told her huskily.

Sara sighed defeatedly. 'And you like her to be happy,' once again this was made plain to her. 'All right, I'll do it. On condition,' she added hardly, 'that you stay away from me.'

'I'll try.'

'You'd better do a damn sight more than that,' she warned. 'Or I'm likely to embarrass you in front of your guests. And you can believe I mean that, Dominic. I never make idle threats.'

'I believe you,' he accepted dully.

'You'd better!' came her parting shot.

As it was she was ten minutes late for her date with Eddie, although he assured her he had only just arrived himself.

'Very flattering!' she grimaced, seating herself opposite him.

He laughed. 'Would you rather I'd sat here waiting for you?'

'No,' she smiled ruefully.

'Don't look now,' he sat forward to whisper, 'but I think we're being watched.'

'Watched?' she frowned in puzzlement.

'Mm, by your future brother-in-law.'

Dominic! 'Where is he?' she asked tautly.

'A few tables back, to your left.'

They were sitting in a quietly exclusive restaurant, but nevertheless Sara knew it wasn't the sort of place Dominic usually frequented. He had followed her here! The waiter was just approaching him for his order, so Sara got hastily to her feet. 'I won't be a minute,' she muttered to Eddie before making her way purposefully over to Dominic.

He waved the waiter away as soon as he saw her approaching him, looking up at her expectantly.

'What the hell do you think you're doing, following me in this way?' Sara lashed out furiously.

'Following you?' he repeated guardedly, curiously pale.

Sara's anger melted at the haggard look of him. 'Go away, Dominic,' she pleaded raggedly. 'I'll see you tonight.'

'You won't let me down?'

'No,' she sighed.

'All right,' he stood up, 'I'll call for you at seven o'clock.' He turned to glance at Eddie. 'I'm glad you didn't kiss him when you arrived,' he said grimly. 'I would probably have punched his face in.'

'Dominic!' she gasped.

He bent to kiss her lightly on the cheek, a gesture perfectly in keeping with her sister's fiancé—if he hadn't unobtrusively caressed the corner of her mouth with the tip of his tongue! His eyes were tortured as he looked down at her. 'Until tonight,' he murmured throatily.

Her eyes flashes deeply brown. 'When there'll be no more of that.'

'No.'

But he didn't sound very convincing. Sara watched him leave the restaurant, half smiling at the arrogant nod he gave Eddie as he walked past their table.

'What's the matter?' Eddie asked as she sat down again. 'Doesn't the high and mighty Dominic Thorne approve of you seeing a mere garage owner?' he derided.

Sara laughed, her tension leaving her. 'It's nothing like that. He wasn't watching us at all, it was just coincidence that he was here.'

'Oh yes?' he scorned. 'When his office is on the other side of London?'

She flushed. 'He's just been to see Marie,' she defended.

'Is he bothering you?' Eddie asked shrewdly.

'Don't be ridiculous!' she snapped, blushing fiery red.

His eyes were narrowed in suspicion. 'Am I being?'

'Very,' she said tightly.

'Okay,' he shrugged. 'Let's order. But if he ever does bother you just let me know and I'll bruise his handsome face a little.'

'Strange,' she drawled with amusement. 'He said the same thing about you,' she explained with a smile.

'Did he now?' his eyebrows rose. 'Maybe I like him after all.'

Sara laughed at the respect in his voice, then changed the subject without being too pointed about it. She had met Eddie a couple of times since her move to live with her father and sister, and usually they went back to her aunt and uncle's house. Today was no exception. She told her aunt of her concern for Marie's headaches.

'Well, I'm sure your father knows best,' her aunt consoled as they made tea and cakes for the two men.

'That's what Dominic says,' Sara sighed.

'Then you must listen to them, dear.'

That was easier said than done, especially when she saw Marie's pale face later that evening. She was dressed to go out with Dominic, and had gone in to see her sister until he arrived.

Marie sat up while she rearranged her pillows for her, her face chalky white, her eyes shadowed. 'I hope I didn't make too much of a fool of myself last night,' she said ruefully.

Sara gently pushed her back against the coolness of the pillows. 'You didn't make a fool of yourself at all,' she reassured her.

'I'm so grateful to you for taking over from me tonight.' Marie put her hand up weakly to her forehead. 'I always feel so washed out after one of these headaches.'

Their father appeared in the doorway. 'I've come to keep you company,' he told Marie. 'Dominic is downstairs, Sara.'

'No, I'm not.' He appeared in the doorway behind their father. 'How are you this evening?' He looked directly at Marie.

'I'm fine.' She patted the bed invitingly beside her.

'I'll wait downstairs,' Sara mumbled, hurriedly kissing her sister on the cheek before rushing out of the room, her head downbent. She collided with Dominic in the doorway, and his strong hands came out to steady her. There was pain in her eyes as she looked up at him, pain that she quickly hid. 'Excuse me,' she said gruffly.

He instantly released her. 'I'll be down in a moment.'

'Take your time.' She forced a lightness into her voice that she didn't feel, very much aware of her father and

Marie. 'I'm in no hurry,' she added, almost running down the stairs.

She was trembling by the time she reached the lounge, knowing that Dominic was probably kissing Marie right at this moment. She was going to be ill herself if she wasn't careful, her appetite having completely deserted her, her nights spent restlessly tossing and turning. And it was all because of this hunger for Dominic!

She had dressed with extra care this evening, had dressed with Dominic in mind if she were honest with herself, and she had to be that, she was deceiving everyone else! She knew perfectly well this evening wouldn't end innocently, knew that before she returned here tonight that she would have spent time in Dominic's arms. And she wasn't able to do a thing about it. He was like a drug in her veins, an addiction she couldn't fight.

Her dress was knee-length, Japanese in style, made of a silky blue material, its very demureness making it very sexy, with its provocative split up the side of her left leg, the narrow styling showing off her pert uptilted breasts and narrow waist, fitting neatly over her bottom and thighs. Her hair was secured loosely on top of her head, her only jewellery the pair of gold stud ear-rings her mother and Richard had given her for Christmas two years ago.

She looked up guiltily as her father entered the room, blushing under his searching gaze. Oh, God, she thought, don't let him guess I love Dominic, don't let him guess!

'I hope we haven't ruined any of your own plans for this evening,' he said.

Sara almost laughed with relief. Her father had put her behaviour down to an altogether different reason than her love for Dominic and her jealousy of Marie. 'Not at all,' she answered smoothly.

'Oh, good,' he seemed relieved. 'Only you seemed a little—upset.'

'No,' she shook her head, 'just nervous. I know how

important this dinner party is to you and Dominic.'

'Not that important that you have to worry yourself about it.' He put his arm about her shoulders. 'Just be yourself, Sara. You'll like Martha and Jim, they're a nice couple.'

Sara frowned. 'Will they be the only people there?'

'Mm. Jim's thinking of giving us a contract to supply equipment to all his British offices. One look at you and he won't hesitate to offer us that contract.' He smiled down at her affectionately.

'Do I look all right?' she asked worriedly. She had dressed with a party in mind, albeit a dinner party, but a quiet evening for four was another matter.

'You look beautiful, doesn't she, Dominic?' he asked the other man as he came into the room.

'Very lovely,' Dominic confirmed, the intensity of his gaze making her blush. 'We should be going,' he said abruptly.

'Have a nice time, darling.' Her father bent to kiss her. 'Don't keep her too late, Dominic. I've noticed she's looking a little pale lately.'

Sara bit her lip, as she led the way out to Dominic's car parked in the driveway. So her father had noticed her pallor too. He mustn't ever be allowed to guess that it was because of her helpless love for Dominic. Plus there was this added worry of her father, of the illness that everyone knew about but no one discussed. Maybe if they had talked about it Marie wouldn't be in this emotional mess.

There was a man getting out of the car parked next to Dominic's, and he turned to acknowledge them. 'Good evening, Dominic. Marie?' he frowned. 'But I thought——'

'This is Sara, Simon.' Dominic held firmly on to her elbow, opening the car door for her.

The man nodded, a man of possibly forty-five, very tall and distinguished-looking. 'Nice to meet you, Miss Hamille.'

Sara gave him a friendly smile, wondering why Dominic was pushing her into the car and not introducing her to the other man as he should have done. 'Who was that?' she asked once they were on their way.

Dominic shrugged. 'A friend of your father's.'

'What's his name?'

'Simon.'

She frowned. 'I know that, I heard you call him it. But Simon What?'

'Forrester,' he revealed in a stilted voice.

'Should I know him?' The name did sound vaguely familiar.

'No,' Dominic denied abruptly.

'Then why do I feel as if I should?'

'I have no idea.'

'Dominic?' she gave him a searching look. 'Dominic, what are you hiding from me?'

His expression lightened. 'I'm not hiding anything,' he smiled. 'Simon is a friend of your father's, there's nothing to add to that.'

'Isn't there?' she persisted.

'Not a thing.'

Sara didn't know why, but she didn't believe him. He was being deliberately casual, and in the light of their meeting this morning she knew he had to be acting. Simon Forrester was a friend of her father; could that possibly make him a doctor, was that the reason Dominic was being so close-mouthed about him? It seemed to be the logical explanation, so she knew it was no good pursuing the subject of Simon Forrester; everyone, including Dominic, clammed up whenever she tried to approach the subject of her father's illness.

Dominic's apartment covered the whole of the top floor of a huge block of flats, the luxurious fittings of the reception area alone showing her that his apartment was going to be quite something.

When they stepped out of the lift it was to be confronted by the man Sara knew to be Danny, the man who had been kissing Marie the last time she saw him.

He pushed away from his leaning position against the wall, his expression one of aggression as he approached Dominic. 'How dare you keep something like that from me?' he attacked. 'You had no right, Nick. No right——'

'Danny!' The use of the other man's name was a warning. 'I'm not alone,' Dominic reminded him.

'I know that.' The other man's mouth twisted as he looked at Sara. 'You're Marie's sister Sara, aren't you?'

'Yes,' she acknowledged quietly.

Dominic unlocked his apartment door. 'Wait for me inside, Sara,' he instructed abruptly. 'I won't be long,' he added as she hesitated.

'I wouldn't count on that,' Danny snarled.

'You have five minutes, Danny,' Dominic told him firmly. 'After that I'll have you thrown out.'

'Typical! What I have to say could take longer than five minutes,' the other man snapped. 'Telling you what I think of you could take all damned night.'

'All night you don't have, five minutes you do,' Dominic told him grimly.

'I——'

'Sara.' Dominic pointedly held the door open for her. She took his hint, and heard the door firmly close behind her. She could hear their raised voices outside, Dominic's controlled, Danny's very heated, and she wondered what on earth Dominic could have done to have so angered the younger man.

Not that she was particularly worried about Dominic's welfare; he was perfectly capable of taking care of himself, both verbally and physically. But Danny had been angry, extremely so. Dominic might have been just as angry if he had known the other man was in the habit of kissing his fiancée.

The apartment was as she had imagined it to be, luxurious, expensive and totally male. It was a typical bachelor home, clean, uncluttered, and obviously kept that way by a daily woman or housekeeper. It turned out to be the latter, a small bustly woman setting the table in the dining-room.

Sara ducked back into the lounge before the woman saw her. Marie would obviously have visited Dominic here, and she didn't feel up to explaining to the housekeeper that she wasn't Marie.

She was sitting in one of the armchairs when Dominic entered the apartment, and instantly stood to her feet to look him over for damage. He didn't appear to be hurt, as he moved to the array of drinks displayed on the side-table and poured himself out a large shot of brandy.

He turned to her after swallowing most of the fiery liquid. 'Would you like anything to drink?' he asked grimly.

'No, thanks. Has he gone?'

'Yes.' Dominic's eyes were narrowed, his expression stern. 'Yes,' he sighed, finishing the brandy in his glass, 'he's gone.'

Sara frowned. 'What did he want?'

He seemed to withdraw from her. 'Nothing important.'

'Nothing important!' she scorned. 'I thought he was going to kill you!'

His mouth twisted. 'Nothing so melodramatic. I'll admit Danny was a little annoyed with me——'

'Annoyed? He was furious!' she persisted.

Dominic shrugged. 'My brother is always furious about something, he always has been.'

Sara paled. 'Your—your brother?'

'Yes,' he bit out grimly. 'Danny is my younger brother, didn't you know that?'

No, she hadn't known that. What she did know was that Dominic's own brother was in love with Marie.

CHAPTER EIGHT

'I—ER—I didn't know.' She licked her lips. 'We didn't get to meet at your mother's the other evening.'

'You didn't miss much,' Dominic dismissed scathingly.

'I'm sure that when he isn't angry he can be very nice,' she said primly.

His eyes blazed. 'Yes, Danny can be charming when he wants to be. Were you attracted to him?' he demanded tautly.

Sara gasped. 'Of course not!'

'Why not?' He slammed his empty glass down on the table-top. 'He's young, presentable—and free!'

'Ah yes, he's free,' she taunted him, seeing the rigid anger in his body. 'Perhaps you could introduce me to him some time, when he isn't quite so angry. Hmm?'

Dominic went white. 'No, I damn well can't!' he exploded, pulling her towards him. 'You aren't going out with Danny, Sara. Over my dead body will you go out with him!'

Once again she had woken the sleeping tiger; Dominic was now shaking with fury. He didn't like the idea that she might date his brother, and his jealousy gave her a warm glow.

'Only joking, Dominic,' she murmured huskily. 'I was only joking,' she smiled, gently touching his rigid cheek.

He clasped her hand in his, taking it to his mouth to feverishly kiss her palm. 'Don't tease, Sara,' he groaned. 'Not about something like that. As far as you're concerned I have a very low pain level.' The doorbell rang. 'Hell!' Dominic muttered. 'That will be Jim and Martha.'

Sara moved deftly away from him as she heard the

housekeeper coming to answer the door. 'I'm not interested in your brother, Dominic,' she assured him softly. 'Although I'm willing to like him simply because he is your brother.'

His tension started to ease. 'Not too much,' he advised huskily. 'He had a thing for Marie last year, he might consider you're a suitable replacement.'

She flinched away from him. 'Like you do?' she said bitterly.

'Sara——'

'Your guests, Dominic.' She turned as the middle-aged couple were shown into the room.

On the whole the evening was a success, although Dominic's brooding attention on her wasn't conducive to helping business along. She eventually suggested showing Martha Jarvis the view from the balcony as a means of leaving Dominic alone with Jim.

It was a magnificent view, the whole of London spread before them like a huge lighted carpet, beautiful and dreamlike.

'It always looks so different like this,' Martha smiled, a still attractive woman of about fifty. She and her husband came from the North of England, and they obviously missed their daughter and grandson whenever they travelled on business, talking of them constantly.

'Even likeable?' Sara teased, knowing that the other couple believed there was nowhere as nice as their beloved North.

Martha goodnaturedly accepted her teasing. 'I like the shops, but that's about all I can say in London's favour.' She wrinkled her nose. 'It's a big, dirty place, where people don't have time for each other.'

Considering that Sara had heard that Northerners were among the most dour people of England she found this comment amazing. Still, who was she to question its validity, having lived in America most of her life?

'I like it,' she shrugged.

Martha touched her arm. 'You'll have to get Dominic to bring you up to visit us some time. You'll see, the North's best.'

'You forget,' Sara said stiffly, 'it's my sister who is marrying Dominic.'

'So it is,' the other woman tutted at her stupidity. 'Still, that's no reason why you shouldn't come with them. I have a son who would be just right for you,' she added conspiratorially.

Sara opened the balcony doors for them to go back inside, laughing at Martha's matchmaking. 'Maybe,' she grinned. 'But would I be right for him?'

'For who?' Dominic asked sharply as they entered the lounge.

'For my son,' Martha told him as she sat down. 'I've been trying to persuade Sara to come and visit us and meet my son John,' she explained lightly.

Sara held her breath at Dominic's darkening expression. 'I doubt I'll have the time,' she put in hastily. 'Although I thank you for the offer,' she smiled at the other couple.

Jim looked at his watch. 'Time we were going, Mother.' He stood up, holding out his hand to a now standing Dominic. 'We've had a grand time, lad. I'll be in touch with you about that contract.'

Sara stood beside Dominic as they made their goodbyes, smiling to herself as she turned back into his apartment.

Dominic followed her, scowling heavily. 'What's so funny?'

She was laughing openly now. 'I just wondered how long it is since you were called "lad".'

He returned her smile ruefully. 'At thirty-five I'm a little old for that, hmm?'

She sat down, curling her legs up beneath her on the sofa. 'Not to a man of fifty-five,' she grinned.

Dominic joined her on the sofa, his long legs stretched out in front of him. 'We got the contract, by the way.'

'I gathered.'

'What was that about the Jarvises' son?'

'Just a mother's usual interest in her son's love-life,' she dismissed. 'No threat to you, Dominic, I can assure you.'

His eyes were deeply blue as he looked at her. 'What does that mean, Sara?' he asked softly.

She drew a ragged breath. 'What do you think it means?'

He swallowed hard, a pulse beating rapidly at his jawline, his hands clenched into fists. 'I—I'm afraid to think,' he groaned.

'Try,' she encouraged throatily.

'God, I love you!' he burst out, straining her to him.

Sara froze. 'Wh—what did you say?' she gulped, not believing her own hearing, wanting to be sure she wasn't hallucinating—could you get high on one glass of wine?

'I love you,' his lips were at her earlobe, nibbling along the sensitive cord in her throat. 'God, how I love you!' He claimed her lips in a fiery kiss.

Love—Dominic *loved* her! She kissed him back with all the love there was inside her, losing herself in the sensation of loving and being loved in return. Her mouth opened to his, their lips moving over each other's as if starved.

'Tell me,' he groaned feverishly. 'Tell me you love me!'

How could she deny the truth? 'I love you,' she breathed against his mouth. 'I love you very much.'

'Then that's all that matters, all that can matter.' He stood up to gather her in his arms and stride through to his bedroom. 'I want you, Sara,' he told her deeply.

Her head rested on his shoulder. 'Yes.'

'Yes—what?' He seemed almost afraid to breathe.

'Thank you?' she quirked one eyebrow, trembling.

The tension between them didn't lessen at her levity, more it seemed to deepen, as Dominic gently laid her down on the bed to look down at her almost reverently.

'What do you want, Sara?' The pulse at his jaw was beating even more rapidly as he waited for her answer.

'You,' she told him simply.

He closed his eyes, shuddering as he fought for control. 'Are you sure?' he asked almost inaudibly.

She raised her hand to smooth the hair at his temple, saddened at the extra grey hair she found there. 'I'm very sure, Dominic.' She met his gaze unflinchingly.

'Then so be it!' He sank down on the bed beside her, ravishing her mouth with his, probing her lips farther apart with the sensuous tip of his tonge, running it along the sensitive area of her inner lip.

Sara was trembling with excitement, her hands tangled in the dark length of his hair, massaging his scalp when she found he liked it, groaned with the pleasure of it. Over the next heated few minutes she discovered several other places of pleasure that excited him, her teeth nibbling his neck and causing him to shake.

'Undress me, Sara.' He lay back invitingly.

She needed no second bidding, and knelt beside him to slowly unbutton his shirt, having already discarded his jacket. His chest was tautly muscled, liberally sprinkled with dark hair, soft and silky to her touch.

She gasped as she felt Dominic's lips on her thigh, the slit up the side of her dress giving him easy access to her silky skin. Her hands travelled over the tautness of his back, her nails digging painfully into his muscled flesh as his hands caressed her inner thigh.

'I can't do anything when you do that,' she collapsed on his chest.

Dominic pulled her on top of him, a hand either side of her face as he gazed deeply into her eyes. 'I go wild just looking at you,' he told her huskily. 'I want to take this slowly, love you as you deserve to be loved, but I'm not sure I'll be able to control this,' he admitted shakily.

Sara knew what this admission cost him, and it only made her love him all the more. She hugged him, her face buried in his throat as she cried for joy. 'Let's get undressed sensibly,' she murmured against his warm skin, 'or else I'm likely to rip your clothes off you.'

Her teasing eased the heated tension between them, and Dominic shook with laughter. He gently moved her up from him. 'Okay—you first,' he requested, his eyes warm on her flushed cheeks.

'I meant together!' she gasped her dismay.

'I know what you meant, but it's more fun this way.'

'I wouldn't know,' she said in a stilted voice, and moved to unzip her dress, all the time wondering how many other women had stripped for him in this very same way. Hundreds, no doubt. And how many of them had he told that he loved them? a traitorous voice asked. None of them, she told herself firmly, as she stepped out of her dress, wearing only a pair of minute briefs, ironically with 'LOVE' embroidered across them! She hadn't dreamt when she had dressed this evening that Dominic would see her like this.

'Sara?' He knelt on the bed in front of her, bare to the waist himself, his chest strong and muscled, his stomach taut and flat, his silky hair growing down his chest, over his navel, and provocatively lower. 'Sara, will this be the first time for you?' He held her firmly in front of him.

She licked her lips nervously. No man liked inexperience in this day and age. She gave a casual shrug of her shoulders. 'Of course not,' she lied lightly.

'Sara!' He shook her gently. 'I'll be able to tell, you know.'

Not if she stopped herself from crying out he wouldn't! 'I'm sorry if you're disappointed, Dominic,' she was deliberately nonchalant, 'but you'll be far from the first.'

'I'm glad,' he gathered her into his arms. 'Loving you is one thing, taking your innocence from you is something I just couldn't do.'

Thank God she had lied! She couldn't be denied

knowing his full possession now, as she removed her last article of clothing to stand before him naked. She was well above average height, her breasts proudly erect, her nipples a deep rose pink, her waist slender, her hips perfectly shaped, her legs long and supple. She watched Dominic shyly from beneath lowered lashes, doing her best to gauge his reaction, wondering if she compared favourably with the other women he had made love to.

He said nothing for several long painful minutes. 'You're the most beautiful, desirable woman I've ever seen in my life,' he told her in awe.

She began to breathe again, throwing herself into his arms. 'That was exactly the right thing to say,' she told him tearfully.

He smoothed her tears away with his thumb-tips. 'The truth often is,' he said huskily. 'You are beautiful, all of you.'

'So are you,' she told him shyly.

'You haven't seen all of me yet.' He firmly sat her down on the bed, his hand going to his belted waist. 'But you will.'

Sara felt that she stopped breathing as he stepped out of his trousers, a pair of navy blue briefs now his only clothing, his thighs powerfully muscled. At the last moment her courage deserted her and she turned away to climb beneath the covering of the sheets, their coolness soothing against her heated flesh.

'Do you want the light on or off?'

She looked up, then quickly looked away again, her face fiery red, that one brief glimpse of Dominic's naked flesh showing her what a truly magnificent body he had, strong and powerful, clearly wanting her as badly as she wanted him. 'Off, please,' she croaked, hoping she wouldn't prove a disappointment to him.

The room was instantly put into darkness, temporarily blinding Sara, and making Dominic a mere shadow. The bedclothes were thrown back as he joined her on the bed, his mouth instantly claiming hers. She relaxed against the hard demand of him, gasping as his hand moved to claim her breast, caressing the nipple to hardness with the tip of his thumb, moving slowly down her body to claim her other breast with his pleasure-giving lips and tongue.

Excitement such as Sara had never known existed coursed through her body, as Dominic's leg moved over hers to trap her to the bed as she would have struggled against that pleasure. It was too much, driving her into ecstasies, making her gasp, cry out as it became unbearable.

Dominic raised his head, his expression one of puzzlement. 'It's all right, darling,' he soothed, sweeping her hair back from her face. 'Calm down, sweetheart.'

She swallowed hard, the tension easing as he gently caressed her. 'I—I'm sorry, Dominic,' she bit her lip. 'I'm just—It's——'

'You're a virgin, aren't you!' he realised tautly.

'It's obvious, is it?' she asked with dread.

His answer was to get off the bed, pulling on a towelling robe before switching on the light. 'Yes, it's obvious,' he confirmed abruptly.

'It matters, doesn't it?' She held the sheet up over her breasts, still throbbing from the touch of his lips.

'Of course it matters!' The lover of minutes ago was completely erased.

'But why?' she cried out her puzzlement. 'When we're married——'

'Married!' he repeated harshly. 'We aren't getting married, Sara.'

'We—we aren't?'

'I'm engaged to Marie!'

'Yes, but——'

'And I'm going to stay that way,' he told her coldly.

'But you said you loved me!'

'And I do,' he groaned.

She blinked dazedly, as she felt her world collapsing about her. 'But you're still going to marry Marie?'

'Yes!' he hissed. 'I wish I could make you understand——'

'You can't,' she choked, getting out of bed to dress hurriedly. 'I've been a fool. I thought loving me meant you wanted to be with me, for all time. But I guess Eddie was right about you from the first,' she added bitterly, leaving her hair loose in her hurry to leave.

Dominic's eyes were glacial. 'Eddie?' he echoed sharply.

'Yes,' her head went back challengingly. 'That first evening we met, when you thought I was Marie, I asked Eddie about you. He told me then exactly what sort of man you are.'

'Considering he's never met me that's quite something!'

Her look was contemptuous. 'People like you don't need to be known. He told me then that one day you intended owning all the business, and that by marrying Marie you would have it. And now you've proved that. You say you love me—if you even know what that word means—and yet you still intend to marry Marie, my father's heiress.'

Dominic had gone white beneath his tan, his eyes blazing. 'You're forgetting something,' he snapped harshly. 'Your father now has two daughters.'

'And you've been trying to bed both of them! You're a bastard, Dominic Thorne, and you can forget what I ever said about loving you! Right now I loathe and despise you, and I doubt that opinion will ever change!' She flounced out of the bedroom, and continued on out of the apartment, hiring a taxi to take her home.

The drive to her father's house seemed never-ending as she sat in hunched-up misery on the back seat of the taxi, her love and belief in Dominic in ruins about her feet. He had been using her, making her a pawn in his ugly game—and how easily she had fallen for it!

But never again, never again would she listen to his words of love or passion. If he could betray her father and Marie after having known them for the past ten years, then he would have no compunction about exploiting her own attraction to him. It must have been obvious to him from the first, and how useful it could have been to him. But she had ruined his plan, hadn't been besotted enough with him to still want to sleep with him after she had found out he still intended marrying Marie. Admittedly he hadn't been corrupt enough to pursue his seduction once he realised her innocence, but she had no doubt he would have overcome those *scruples* given time. He had wanted her completely and utterly in love with him, agreeable to his every whim. What a pity for him that he had failed!

It made her wonder what he could have done to Danny, his own brother, to make him want to attack him in that way. Danny had accused him of something; could it possibly be that he had finally found the courage to stand up to his brother about his engagement to Marie, to tell Dominic of his own love for her? To think that Dominic had gone that far, dazzled and captured Marie from his own brother merely for his own mercenary ends. The thought disgusted her. And what disgusted her more was that she had almost been a victim of his lethal charm herself.

To her dismay she wasn't to be allowed to escape to the privacy of her bedroom to wallow in her misery. Marie's bedroom light was on, and she called Sara in to speak to her.

'You should be asleep,' Sara scolded, sitting down on the side of the bed.

'Ssh!' Marie smiled mischievously. 'Daddy doesn't know I'm still awake.'

'You're feeling better?'

'I was feeling better this afternoon,' her sister admitted with a grin, 'but I hate these business dinners of Dominic's.'

'I wish I'd known earlier,' Sara groaned. 'Headache or no headache, you would have gone.'

'Was it ghastly?'

'Yes! No.' She shrugged. 'Not really.' Only the latter part of it!

'I promise I won't land you in it again,' Marie giggled. 'I just didn't feel like being entertaining this evening.'

'I'll let you off this time.' Sara frowned, remembering something that had been troubling her. 'Marie, tonight when—when Dominic and I were leaving a man was just arriving. I think Dominic said his name was Simon Forrester.'

'Simon?' Marie's voice sharp.

'Yes,' Sara watched her closely. 'Dominic said he was a friend of Dad's.'

'That's right, he is,' her sister answered with obvious relief.

Sara bit her lip, deciding to take a shot in the dark and see if it paid off. 'He also said he was a doctor.' She watched Marie's reaction, seeing her blanch.

'Yes, he is,' Marie's tone was brittle. 'Does it matter?'

'Not really,' Sara replied casually. 'I just wondered whether he was here professionally or socially.'

Marie began to pleat the sheet between nervous fingers. 'Why on earth should he be here professionally?'

'I thought perhaps because of your headaches ...' She had thought no such thing. If Simon Forrester had been here professionally then it had been to see her father, and conveniently when she was out of the house.

'No,' Marie denied instantly. 'I'm feeling rather tired, Sara, perhaps I should go to sleep now.'

'Yes, of course.' She stood up. 'I'll see you in the morning.' She bent to kiss her sister goodnight.

But she didn't sleep once she reached her bedroom, too disturbed by the evening's events to be able to relax enough for that. She had been stupid tonight, more stupid than she had ever been before in her life. She was ashamed of herself for being taken in so easily. But the reason she had been taken in still existed—she still loved Dominic!

How could she love such a despicable man, a man who was marrying her own sister for mercenary reasons? Maybe he did love Marie, maybe he loved her too, but it made no difference to his plans to be the sole owner of the business he and her father now ran jointly.

And tomorrow, or the day after, she was going to have to face Dominic again, put on a show so that he wouldn't guess how much he had hurt her. After what she had said to him she doubted she would have to fight any attempts on his part to kiss or touch her.

She didn't give him the chance the next day, spending the whole day with her aunt, telephoning Eddie and going out with him that evening. He was the uncomplicated companion she needed at the moment.

There was no sign of Dominic when she finally arrived home, so she entered the house with a light heart. After crying herself to sleep the night before she had spent the day pushing Dominic firmly to the back of her mind, and the last thing she wanted was to run into him now. Eddie had given her her confidence back in herself with his lighthearted flirting, receiving a casual kiss goodnight to his surprise. Purely sisterly, she had assured him with a laugh.

The butler came to remove her coat once she got in. 'Mr Thorne has been calling you all day, Miss Sara,' he informed her.

She stiffened, frowning. 'Did he leave a message?' She did her best to remain calm.

'No, Miss Sara, although I think he wanted to talk to you quite urgently. He's gone away on business for several days, but he said he would call you again as soon as he could.'

'I didn't realise he was going away. Wasn't he here this evening, Granger?'

For a moment he looked puzzled. 'I think you may have misunderstood me, Miss Sara. I didn't mean Mr Dominic Thorne, I meant Mr Daniel Thorne.'

'Danny?' she echoed sharply. What on earth could Danny want with her?

'That's right,' the butler nodded.

'Are you sure he wanted me, Granger?'

'Very sure, Miss Sara.'

'Did he mention where he was going?'

'Germany,' he supplied. 'And he wasn't sure when he would be returning.'

'Thank you,' she said absently. 'I—If he calls again, let me know immediately, won't you?'

'Of course, Miss Sara.'

Why could Danny want to see her? They had met briefly last night for the first time, very briefly, and he hadn't seemed that desperate to talk to her then.

He didn't call again, his business in Germany was probably keeping him fully occupied. And she didn't see or hear from Dominic either, although she knew he and Marie met most evenings. Perhaps her message had gone home, whatever the reason he left her alone.

'We're going shopping,' Marie announced on Saturday morning as the two of them breakfasted together.

'We are?' Sara asked tolerantly.

'Yes,' her sister nodded. 'Well, it isn't shopping exactly,' she added a little guiltily. 'I know where we're going, and I've already bought the—whatever it is we want. We just have to pick them—it up.'

'Marie . . .?' Sara eyed her suspiciously. 'What have you been up to?'

'Nothing. It's a surprise. For you!' She could hardly contain her excitement. 'Have you finished?' she tried to hurry Sara's breakfast along.

'No, I haven't.' Sara refused to be rushed, slowly sipping her coffee.

'Yes, you have.' Marie took the cup out of her hand, standing up expectantly.

Sara didn't move. 'What about the party tonight? Shouldn't we be doing something towards that this morning?'

'It's all arranged. Everything will be arriving this afternoon. Anyway, Granger is perfectly capable of dealing with any hitches that may arise.'

'He wasn't yesterday when you couldn't be spared to help me tidy Dad's study,' Sara reminded her ruefully.

Marie grinned. 'I've been doing it for years, simply because Daddy won't let the staff go in there. I thought it was time you took a turn.'

'And you were very conveniently busy with other things,' Sara said dryly.

'Very conveniently,' Marie grinned.

The dress salon wasn't exactly a surprise to Sara, she had half expected it. Marie hadn't been out and bought a new dress for the party yet, so it followed that today she was going to get one. Only she had gone one step further, she had had identical dresses designed!

'Aren't they lovely!' she cried ecstatically as they were brought out for their approval.

They were indeed lovely, but *identical*!

'At the time you ordered two dresses the same,' the saleswoman gushed. 'I admit to being rather puzzled. But now ...' she waved her arms in their direction pointedly, 'now I understand.'

Sara wished she did. 'No one will be able to tell us apart,' she complained.

'That's the whole idea!' Marie was flushed with pleasure at her idea. 'Let's fit them on.'

'Marie——'

'Come on, Sara!' She dragged her towards the changing rooms.

The dress fitted her as if it had been made for her, but then it should, it had been modelled on Marie! It was black chiffon, a colour she didn't usually wear, very simple in design, its very simplicity its main attraction, strapless, held above the breasts only by their pertness, fitted over the bust to be caught in at the waist, flowing out in several layers of chiffon to her feet. It was beautiful, gave her added maturity and sophistication, and she could see it did the same for Marie when they met minutes later.

'My goodness!' the saleswoman gasped. 'You look like mirror images!'

'Don't we! Don't we, Sara?' Marie pleaded for her approval.

Sara sighed. 'Yes, we do. But we're going to cause a lot of confusion at this party tonight.'

Marie smiled her glee. 'That's the whole idea.'

The first person to fall foul of their little trick was their father, who stared at them in utter confusion when they joined him in the lounge before their guests arrived.

'Clever,' he smiled, putting an arm around each of them and holding them to his sides. 'Sara,' he turned to kiss her. 'Marie,' he turned to kiss her.

Marie pouted her disappointment. 'You guessed!'

He laughed. 'I cheated. I can tell by the perfumes you wear,' he explained.

Marie brightened. 'You couldn't tell otherwise.'

'No,' he answered solemnly.

'Sure?'

'Sure,' he nodded.

Dominic was the first to arrive, and his eyes narrowed as he looked at them both. 'I seem to have played this scene before,' he murmured. 'I'm supposed to guess which one to kiss. Right?'

Marie nodded, having extreme difficulty not speaking and so giving away her identity.

It was the first time Sara had seen him since the night at his apartment, and she noticed that he looked drawn and tired, despite his forced smile. Perhaps his conscience had been bothering her; she hoped so.

This time he didn't even hesitate, but walked straight over to Marie and kissed her confidently on the lips.

This didn't please her at all, and she glared up at him. 'You weren't supposed to guess!'

He raised his eyebrows. 'You would rather I kissed Sara?'

'Yes—I mean no.' She sighed. 'How did you know which one was me?'

'Shouldn't I know the girl I'm going to marry?'

'I suppose so,' she accepted ruefully. 'But I bet Sara's disappointed that you guessed right.'

Sara gasped, turning fiery red. Could Marie possibly have guessed that she had been kissed by Dominic many times before?

Dominic turned glacial blue eyes on her. 'Are you?' he asked coldly.

Her head went back, her mouth tight. 'Not at all. I have my own boy-friend arriving shortly. I'm sure he'll be only too pleased to supply as many kisses as I want.'

'Eddie?' he rasped tautly.

'Of course.' She made her tone appear light, aware of her father and Marie even if Dominic wasn't.

His mouth twisted. 'Of course.' He turned away.

Once the guests began to arrive, exclaiming over how alike the two girls were—as if they wouldn't be when they were identical twins!—she was able to push Dominic to the back of her subconscious, vaguely aware of his being in the room, even feeling his gaze on her on occasion, but making no effort to return it.

Eddie was enjoying himself immensely, his arm loosely about her waist in casual possession. 'Is he rising to the bait yet?' he bent to whisper in her ear.

Sara frowned up at him. 'What are you talking about?'

'Not what, who. And it's Dominic Thorne,' he grinned. 'He's been glaring at me for the last ten minutes.'

An involuntary movement had her facing in Dominic's direction, to find herself looking straight into his narrowed blue eyes. Yes, he was staring at them, not just looking, but staring straight at them, and making no effort to look as if he were doing anything else. Her answer was to stand on tiptoe and kiss Eddie firmly on the mouth. When she glanced back at Dominic he was no longer looking their way, although he was slightly pale under his tan, his mouth set in a rigid line.

'I liked that,' Eddie murmured. 'But not the reason behind it.' He gave her a reproachful look.

Sara blinked hard. 'I don't know what you mean.'

His fingers pinched in at her waist. 'Liar,' he whispered close to her ear. 'But I'll forgive you this time. Just stop putting the poor man through the hoops.'

'Eddie——'

'I know,' he interrupted her warning tone. 'Mind my own business. The way he keeps looking at me it could become my business any moment now. He looks ready to hit me!'

Her eyes sparkled angrily. 'He has no right!'

'That isn't what your pulse rate is telling me,' Eddie taunted.

She glared up at him. 'That's just anger.'

He laughed softly. 'Of course it is,' he mocked. 'Who on earth is that woman talking to Aunt Susan?'

Sara followed his line of vision, and her mouth quirked into a smile. 'That's Cynthia Robotham-James,' she said with humour. 'The woman who gave the party Pete took me to,' she explained.

'Pete's still interested in photographing you, you know. He would love to work with you.'

'Well, he's going to be disappointed. I think we should go and save Aunt Susan,' she grimaced. 'Cynthia tends to be a bit overwhelming. On second thoughts,' she saw Danny Thorne just arriving, 'you go and rescue her, there's someone over there I have to talk to.'

'I see.' Eddie saw her looking at Danny. 'In that case I'll go and console myself with Cynthia.'

Sara spluttered with laughter. 'Good luck!'

'I'll need it, she could probably eat me for breakfast.'

'And not even know it!' she taunted.

'Cheeky! Just because you don't fancy me it doesn't

mean I'm unattractive to women.' He straightened his cuff. 'I'll go over there and captivate her with my charm.'

The last Sara saw of him he wasn't doing a bad job of it, Aunt Susan smiling with obvious relief as Eddie drew Cynthia's attention away from her.

Danny was searching the crowds of people at the party, stopping when he saw her walking towards him.

'It's Sara,' she told him before she could be an unwilling witness to any embarrassing declarations of love on his part.

'I know,' he nodded. 'I have to talk to you.'

She didn't question his knowing her identity. If he loved Marie he was probably able to tell she wasn't her as well as Dominic had. 'Perhaps my father's study . . .?' she suggested.

'That will do.' He seemed charged with a nervous energy, sparing not a glance for the other people at the party as he led the way out of the room.

Sara shut the study door after them, instantly shutting out the noise. 'Now what did you want to talk to me about?'

'Marie,' Danny said heavily, his eyes dark with pain.

He was going to try and enlist her help in getting Marie for himself! She shook her head. 'There's nothing I can do.'

His expression became fierce. 'There must be something someone can do! I can't just sit back and let Marie die!'

Sara looked at him dazedly, clutching on to the back of the chair for support. 'Wh—what did——' she swallowed hard. 'What did you say?' she asked shakily.

Danny avidly searched her face, shaking his head. 'My God,' he groaned, closing his eyes, 'you didn't know, did you? No one told you Marie is dying!'

CHAPTER NINE

'I DON'T believe you!' Sara choked. 'You're lying!' Her voice rose hysterically and her legs began to shake, finally giving out on her as she collapsed to the floor, her eyes huge in her white face. 'Tell me you're lying,' she pleaded tearfully, numb with shock.

Danny came down on the floor beside her, pulling her into his arms. 'I'm not lying, Sara,' he murmured into her hair.

She shook against him. 'But why? How?'

'I would have thought the "why" was obvious,' a steely voice interrupted them. 'The "how" should be equally obvious,' Dominic added contemptuously.

Danny turned to look at his brother. 'Shut your filthy mouth!' he snapped.

Dominic raised his eyebrows. 'Perhaps if you both got up off the floor I just might be able to do that.'

Danny sprang to his feet, his expression fierce. 'What the hell are you saying now?'

His brother closed the study door and came further into the room. 'If the two of you have to sneak off together at least choose somewhere a little more private—and comfortable—for your lovemaking.'

'No, Danny!' Sara screamed as he flew at Dominic, his fist landing on his brother's chin.

Dominic's face darkened with an anger even fiercer than Danny's. 'You'll never know how glad I am that you did that,' he muttered through bared teeth. 'I only needed the excuse to hit you . . .'

Sara closed her eyes to shut out the sight of Dominic beating his brother to a pulp. The furniture was flying everywhere as first one man and then the other fell across the desk or against the chair. Sara couldn't make a move to stop them, although she did manage to pull herself to the corner of the room out of harm's way.

'That's enough.' Danny leant against the side of the desk, trying in vain to staunch the flow of blood from his nose.

'More than enough,' Dominic agreed grimly, a trickle of blood escaping from the cut on his mouth. 'Get out of here. And don't come near Sara again,' he added threateningly.

Danny looked stricken as he turned towards her, seeing her sitting wide-eyed and shocked in the corner of the room, and went down on his haunches to her, helping her to her feet. 'Stop it, Dominic,' he warned as the other man made a savage movement towards him. 'Can't you see the state she's in?' He sat her down in a chair, rubbing her chilled hands.

If anything Dominic's expression darkened even more. 'Were you forcing yourself on her?' he demanded tautly. 'Because if you were——'

'Shut up, Dominic,' Danny sighed, all the time dabbing at his bleeding nose. 'Sara has just received the biggest shock of her life.'

His eyes narrowed sharply. 'My God, you didn't——'

'Yes!' Danny hissed. 'Someone should have told me that even Marie's sister didn't know.'

'You stupid——! My God, you're going to answer to me later for this!' Dominic exploded. 'In the meantime you'd better get to a hospital and get something done about your nose.'

'But Sara——'

'Will be perfectly safe with me,' he interrupted grimly. 'Just get the hell out of here, Danny. I think you've caused enough trouble for one day.'

'How was I supposed to know Sara hadn't been told? I naturally assumed——'

'We would hardly come out and baldly tell her something like that. In time——'

'In time!' Sara repeated shrilly, suddenly coming to

life, looking up at Dominic with accusing eyes. '*In time* you and my father were going to tell me Marie is dying, that having found my twin I'm now going to lose her again! And how much *time* was it going to take for you to tell me—on her deathbed, perhaps?' Her voice broke emotionally.

Dominic looked at his brother. 'My God, you did a good job of this!'

'Don't blame him,' Sara snapped. 'Maybe his method wasn't very tactful, but at least he considered me adult enough to *be* told.'

'Would you please leave us, Danny?' Dominic said tautly.

'Sara?'

She looked at Dominic's set, rigid features. 'Yes, go, Danny. You really should get your nose seen to.' It was still bleeding.

He grimaced. 'I think it's broken,' he muttered as he left.

'Sara——'

She shook off Dominic's hand, standing up and moving away from him. 'Don't touch me!' she spat the words at him. 'Don't ever touch me again. Just tell me, tell me what's wrong with Marie.'

He licked the blood from his lip. 'Perhaps your father——'

'No, *you*!' she told him heatedly. 'I want you to tell me.'

He sighed. 'Then perhaps we should sit down. This could take some time, and you've already received enough of a shock.'

Sara sat. 'I'm waiting,' she said in a cold voice.

'You know that Marie fell down the stairs about six months ago,' he began.

She nodded. 'The same day I had my accident.'

'Yes. Well, that fall did more than cause a bump on the head and a twisted ankle.'

'What else?' she asked dully.

'Shortly after falling Marie began to have excruciating pains in the head, so severe that she would cry out with the agony of them.'

'She still gets them,' Sara recalled tightly.

Dominic frowned. 'That bad?'

'Yes.'

He shook his head. 'She said they were getting better.'

Her mouth twisted. 'Perhaps she didn't want to worry you.'

'She eventually went to see a specialist,' Dominic ignored her bitter dig at him. 'Simon Forrester is that specialist.'

God, what a fool she was! All this time she had been blinded by her belief that it was her father who was ill, when all the pointers had really been to its being Marie. Marie was the one with the headaches, the one kept in bed by her illness. She should have realised that Marie was the one her father had told her aunt and uncle was dying, instead she had jumped completely to the wrong conclusion. Was it more painful to lose her sister than her father, could one gauge a loss like that? She couldn't, and she wouldn't even try.

'Why can't Simon Forrester do anything for her?' she demanded to know.

Dominic shrugged. 'Clever as he is he just can't perform miracles. Simon discovered a minute fracture of the skull that wasn't apparent at the time of the accident. That fracture of bone could move at any time and kill her.'

'Can't it be removed?' Sara cried.

'No,' he replied grimly.

'But surely——'

'No!' he repeated tautly. 'It can't.'

'This is absurd! She's young, beautiful, a wonderful person. God couldn't be cruel enough to take her life. Besides, she doesn't look ill,' she added foolishly.

'Believe me, she is.'

'Then why are you marrying her?' Sara turned on him angrily. 'You must have known she was dying when you asked her to marry you—you've only been engaged a few months.'

Dominic's expression was remote, unapproachable. 'My reasons for marrying Marie are my own.'

'And your reason for making love to me?' she asked shrilly. 'Could it be that you decided to have a standby, just in case you didn't get to marry Marie before she dies? After all, one Michael Lindlay daughter is as good as another!' Her head flew back with the force of Dominic's palm against her cheek. She didn't move, looking up at him with lifeless eyes, too numb to even feel the pain he had just inflicted. 'I wouldn't marry you if you got down on your knees and crawled to me across broken glass,' she told him with cold vehemence. 'Just the thought of being in the same room with you makes me feel nauseated!'

Dominic was grey, harsh lines etched into his face. 'Goodbye, Sara,' and he quietly left the room.

As soon as he had left Eddie came in, frowning his concern as his sharp gaze took in her white shocked face, her dishevelled appearance. 'What the hell is going on here?' he asked concernedly. 'World War Three? The two Thorne men have just walked out of here looking as if they've been in battle, one with a bleeding nose, Dominic Thorne looking as if he would like to hit someone.'

'Me,' Sara acknowledged dully. 'He—he's a bastard, Eddie. A cold, heartless, mercenary bastard.' She began to shiver, even though the room was very warm. 'Get me out of here, Eddie,' she cried her desperation. 'Get me away from here!'

'All right, love,' his arm came protectively about her shoulders.

'Out through the french doors. Don't make me see anyone.' She couldn't face all those people in the other room.

He took her to his flat over his garage, a comfortable two-bedroomed flat. He poured her out a glass of whisky, watching while she drank it all down.

'Now,' he sat down, holding her hands in his, 'tell me about it.'

'I—I can't!' she collapsed sobbingly against his chest, knowing she couldn't discuss Marie with him, not until she had spoken to her father and sister. 'I just can't, Eddie!' She looked up at him appealingly.

'All right, love.' He smoothed her hair back with gentle fingers. 'Just sit here with me and don't worry about a thing. No one can touch you here, I won't let them.'

She knew that he wouldn't, felt confident of his ability to protect her. She certainly wasn't able to protect or help herself, her thoughts were all on Marie and the injury that was going to take her from them.

And then there were the terrible things she had said to Dominic, the awful damning things said in the heat of the moment. She couldn't really believe the things she had said to him, had hit out at him because he happened to be there, not because she really *meant* those things.

But he wouldn't know that, and she doubted he would give her the chance to tell him. Besides, she might not believe *that* about him, but he had still made love to her while intending to marry Marie.

When she woke up all was silent about her, the only light in the room from the electric fire Eddie must have switched on while she slept. Her head was resting on the slow rise and fall of his chest, his relaxed pose telling her of his own slumbers.

She moved gingerly, stretched her cramped limbs. 'Sorry,' she said ruefully as Eddie's eyes instantly opened. 'I didn't mean to wake you.'

'You didn't.' He sat up too. 'I wasn't really asleep, just resting.' He looked at her searchingly. 'How do you feel now?'

'Stiff,' she grimaced. 'What time is it?'

'Almost three o'clock,' he supplied.

'Oh, God!' she groaned, putting a hand up to her temple. 'They'll be wondering where I am.'

'No, they won't,' Eddie said quietly. 'I telephoned your father and told him you were with me. He told me everything, Sara,' he added softly.

She at once looked stricken, as the memory of the evening just past came painfully back to her. 'Everything?' she croaked.

He nodded. 'Yes. I told him I would take you home when you're ready.'

Sara shivered. 'I'll never be ready to go back and accept that!'

Eddie's hand covered hers. 'You can't make it go away by ignoring it.'

'She's too young, Eddie,' Sara groaned.

He nodded, compassion in his eyes. 'And she has everything to live for, a father and a sister who love her, and a fiancé who would sacrifice his own happiness to make her happy.'

Sara gave him a sharp look. 'You mean Dominic?'

'Of course.'

'What do you mean?'

He shrugged. 'I mean he likes Marie to be—happy.'

Yes, she knew that! Something else that should have told her it was Marie she was in danger of losing. Dominic was obsessed with seeing that Marie had everything she possibly could to make her happy.

'We all do,' she said huskily.

'But not like he does.'

'Possibly not.' Although it hadn't stopped him trying—no, succeeding, in getting her into bed with him. 'I'd better go, Eddie. My father is probably expecting me.'

He nodded. 'He said he would wait up.'

The light was on in the lounge when she arrived home, despite the lateness of the hour. She hesitated at the front door, looking uncertainly at Eddie.

'You would rather go in alone, hmm?' he guessed shrewdly.

She smiled her relief. 'Thanks, Eddie.' He had been so kind to her she hadn't wanted to tell him she wanted to see her father in private. She reached up and kissed him on the mouth. 'I think I love you,' she whispered huskily.

He touched her gently on the cheek. 'That's what honorary brothers are for. 'Night, love.' He bent and kissed her.

Her father was alone, and stood up as soon as she entered the room. He looked old, defeated and old.

'Oh, Dad!' She launched herself tearfully into his arms, her body shaking with deep racking sobs.

'I know, child. I know.' He stroked her hair, cradling her to him.

'I don't think I can bear it!' she choked.

'We have to, Sara. And we have to be strong, for Marie's sake.'

'I know,' she sniffed, wiping the tears away with the back of her hand. 'Why didn't you tell me, Dad? All this time I thought it was you, and I couldn't understand why you hadn't told me about it.'

'Me?' he frowned. 'Why on earth should you think a thing like that?'

She explained overhearing part of his conversation with her aunt and uncle. 'I'm afraid I jumped to conclusions,' she admitted ruefully. 'It's just that Marie is so young——' she broke off emotionally. 'I'm sorry, this must be worse for you than it is for me.'

'No. I've seen how close the two of you have become the last few weeks, almost as if you've been together all your lives. I'm grateful for that, Sara.' He ran his hand tiredly over his eyes. 'It's made it a little easier for her.'

Sara swallowed hard. 'She—she knows?' remembering the conversation they had had about death she thought she must do.

'Oh yes,' he sighed. 'Not at first. But when the headaches continued,' he shrugged, 'she guessed. She went wild for a few weeks, although that stopped once she became engaged to Dominic.'

But had it? Dominic hadn't seemed surprised when he had thought she was Marie out with another man. He had been angry, but not surprised. Maybe it had happened before. But wouldn't she feel the same way in Marie's place, wouldn't she want to break out too, hit out at the world for taking her young life from her? She knew she would, although their father obviously had no idea of it.

'I'm very grateful to Dominic,' her father continued. 'And sorry for him too. It must be very hard for him knowing the woman he loves is going to die.'

So hard that he occasionally wanted to hold a living, breathing replica of Marie, to make love to her double knowing that she wasn't going to die? She knew with sickening clarity that this was the reason Dominic made love to her, told her he loved her—he had wanted her to be Marie, a Marie who would live.

She licked her dry lips. 'Will they—will they marry—before——'

'I have no idea,' her father revealed heavily. 'I haven't interfered in their plans in any way, either the engagement or wedding plans. If they want to marry they will.'

'But is that fair on Dominic?' It was already obviously tearing him apart now, but if Marie became his wife . . .!

'No,' her father sighed. 'But Dominic has a definite mind of his own.'

She knew that, but at the moment Dominic's mind didn't seem to be functioning rationally. Marie's illness was filling him with a desperation that made him turn to Sara. God, the things she had said to him earlier, how he must hate her for that! No more than she hated herself!

She took a deep breath. 'Is Marie asleep now?'

'Mm,' her father nodded. 'She wanted to wait up with

me, but I wouldn't let her. The party was strain enough for her.'

'I'm sorry to be such a worry to you.' Sara bit her lip.

He put his arm about her shoulders. 'You aren't a worry, Sara, you're part of this family. Maybe we're at fault for not telling you, but that was the way Marie wanted it.'

She frowned. 'Marie didn't want me told?' Somehow that hurt.

'Only because she wanted your reaction to her to be that of any sister towards another. Very few people know of her illness, only myself, Dominic, his mother—and his brother too now.' His mouth twisted.

'I think Danny is in love with her,' Sara revealed huskily.

'I know,' her father acknowledged heavily. 'But it won't do him any good, Marie just isn't interested.'

'No.' Dominic was Marie's love, but Sara felt pity for Danny, knowing such an unwanted love herself, for Dominic. It seemed that both of them had lost out, that they had loved tragically.

She went to bed, but she didn't sleep, and Marie seemed very restless too, tossing and turning in her bed. She went in to look at her once, just to make sure she wasn't awake and in pain. Marie was asleep, but muttering constantly, actually crying out a couple of times. She looked so young and vulnerable lying there, the bright bubbly personality she showed to other people stripped from her, leaving her looking like a lost little girl.

Marie slept in late the next morning. Sara didn't sleep at all, finally giving up to go and sit downstairs. It seemed her father was sleeping late too, and when the maid announced Dominic's arrival she had no other choice but to receive him, her embarrassment acute as she sat up from her lying position on the sofa.

Dominic looked no more pleased to see her than she was him; his expression was forbidding. 'Marie and your father are still resting?' he asked stiffly, looking very tall and attractive in navy blue trousers and a matching fitted shirt, the sleeves of the latter turned back to just below his elbows.

'Yes,' she answered gruffly.

'But you didn't feel the same need?' There was bitter mockery in his voice.

'I—I couldn't sleep.'

'Couldn't, or wasn't allowed to?' Dominic scorned.

Sara was very pale, her brown eyes shadowed. 'What do you mean?'

'You spent the night with your lover, didn't you?' he derided harshly.

She blushed. 'I spent part of the night with Eddie, yes,' she confirmed in a stilted voice. 'But not all of it.'

'At least your father was spared that humiliation.' Dominic's mouth twisted. 'Explaining away your sudden absence wasn't very easy, worrying about what you were doing was even harder on him.'

'What I was doing . . .?' Sara echoed in a choked voice.

'Yes,' he snapped tautly. 'Spending the night with your lover wasn't supposed to be conducive to his peace of mind, was it?'

'Eddie wasn't my lover——'

'Wasn't?' Dominic cut in sharply. 'Does that mean he is now?' He grasped her arms and shook her. 'Does it, Sara?'

'And if he were?' Her eyes blazed with anger. She was exhausted from her sleepless night, crying with the pain of her sister's illness, and aching with the love she felt towards Dominic. Just to have him touch her, even in anger like this, was an agony of pleasure almost too much to bear. She shook out of his grasp, anger her only form of defence against his overwhelming attraction. 'What does it have to do with you?' she asked him defiantly.

He thrust her even further away from him. 'Not a lot,

apparently. What time did you get home? And don't ask what that has to do with me, I just wanted to know what time Marie got to bed.'

There was silent condemnation in his glacial blue eyes, and all fight left her. 'She was already in bed when I got home just after three,' she told him dully.

His mouth tightened. 'Why him, Sara?' he ground out fiercely.

'Why him——? He isn't my lover, Dominic,' she admitted softly. 'I just cried on his shoulder a little.'

'You found his preferable to mine?'

She swallowed hard. 'After what I said to you last night I doubted you would ever talk to me again. Dominic——'

'No more recriminations, Sara,' he advised grimly.

'I wasn't going to accuse, I was going to apologise! What I said to you was unforgivable. You obviously love Marie very much, and I—I'm only sorry I can't be her.' She looked down at her kneading hands.

He drew a ragged breath. 'Sara——'

The lounge door opened noisily to admit Marie. 'Good morning, everyone,' she smiled. 'Dominic!' she reached up and kissed him. 'Sara,' she said more softly, gently kissing her on the cheek. 'All right?' She held Sara's hands.

Tears filled Sara's eyes at her sister's concern, concern for *her*, when she was the one who was dangerously ill. 'I—I'm fine,' she choked. 'I—Oh, God!' she collapsed into Marie's waiting arms, sobbing out her distress. 'I'm sorry,' she moved back seconds later, wiping away her tears. 'This is the last thing you need.'

'I don't mind,' Marie assured her. 'I realise it was a shock for you.'

Sara gave the ghost of a smile. 'Not as much as it must have been for you.'

Her sister shrugged. 'I've got used to it. You will too, in time.'

'Never!' Sara vowed vehemently.

'I hate to interrupt,' Dominic said quietly, 'but my mother is expecting us, Marie.'

'Of course,' she nodded, smiling.

'You—you're going out?' Sara asked dazedly.

Marie moved to Dominic's side. 'I'm not being trite, but life has to go on. I'm lunching with Dominic's mother.'

She nodded. 'Of course. I—I'll see you later, shall I?'

She knew Marie was right, life did have to go on, but for her life was limited—and it didn't seem fair. There had to be something they could do, something *she* could do. She wouldn't let all the life and vitality in Marie die without a fight.

Her father was still asleep, and she didn't want to disturb him. But she wanted Simon Forrester's address, wanted to talk to him about Marie, find out if there really was nothing that could be done for her.

She did something in that moment that she had never done before, she deliberately violated someone else's privacy, looking through the address book on her father's desk in his study, sure that Simon Forrester's address would be in there, it was sure to be somewhere it could be found at all times.

The telephone number was there, but no address, so she called him instead. He might not even be in, it was a Sunday after all, and like most busy men he probably liked to relax on his day off.

The telephone rang only twice before it was picked up. 'Forrester here,' was barked down the telephone.

Oh dear, he didn't sound very happy! 'It's Sara Hamille, Mr Forrester,' she began tentatively.

'Ah yes,' his voice mellowed somewhat. 'You want to see me, hmm?'

'Yes,' she answered dazedly. 'But how did you know?'

'I could say telepathy,' he said in an amused voice. 'But if I did I would be lying. Your father telephoned me last night, so I knew I would hear from you today.

Come over, my dear, and we'll have a little chat about your sister.'

'You're sure I won't be causing you any inconvenience?'

'Not at all,' he said warmly. 'Come over now and we'll have lunch together. I'll expect you in a few minutes.'

She obtained his address and rang off. She hadn't expected him to agree to see her so soon, but she felt grateful that he could, leaving a message with Granger that she would be out to lunch, knowing her father would worry about her when he found her gone.

Simon Forrester's house was impressive, and surely much too big for one man. He probably had a wife and family, although he hadn't given that impression on the telephone.

He had neither wife nor family, and lived in this big house alone. Although he didn't look as if he spent much of his time alone; there was a roguish smile on his lips as he appraised her from head to foot.

'Let's go into the drawing room,' he suggested with a smile, very casually dressed in denims and a light blue shirt, looking nothing like the famous surgeon he undoubtedly was. 'Now, what would you like to know?' he asked once they were both seated.

A direct man himself, Simon Forrester expected her to be equally direct. 'I want to know what you can do to save my sister,' she told him simply.

He raised dark eyebrows. 'And what makes you think I can do anything?'

Her hands wrung together as she sat on the edge of her seat. 'I just know that you can,' she told him with feeling. 'Don't tell me how I know, I just do.'

Simon Forrester nodded. 'Your father told me about this affinity you have with Marie.'

'You don't think it's stupid?'

'Not at all. It often happens with identical twins. You found several similar illnesses that occurred during your childhood, I believe, and yet I'm sure that if you really went into this deeply you would find other similarities. You and Marie are incredibly alike.'

Even down to loving the same man! 'Then there is something you can do for her,' she persisted. 'I just know there is.'

'There is a chance——'

'I knew it!' Her eyes glowed, there was an air of excitement about her.

'A chance neither your father nor Marie is willing to take,' he finished.

Sara frowned. 'I don't understand. Surely any chance is better than none at all?'

Simon Forrester was deadly serious now, his flirtatious air completely gone. 'Not when there's a chance you could be dead, or as good as.'

She went white. 'You mean——'

He stood up to pace the room, as if impatient with his own inability to bring a happy ending to Marie's suffering. 'The brain is the most sensitive organ in the body, the slightest mistake with that and—well, any number of things could happen, and do.'

'You mean she could be paralysed?'

'Or have permanent brain damage,' he nodded.

'Oh, God!' She felt sick. Hope had been given to her only to be taken away again.

'Yes,' he sighed. 'It isn't much of a choice, is it?'

'No.' She swallowed hard, and stood up. 'I think I should be on my way now. I—Thank you for giving me your time.' She couldn't even begin to think about eating lunch now, and she knew Simon Forrester sensed that, as he did not press her at all.

His expression was full of compassion. 'I wish there were some sort of guarantee I could give you that I could bring Marie through an operation of this kind, but unfortunately that isn't possible. Marie claims she would rather die than be imperfect in that way. In a way I can understand that—brain damage, of any kind, isn't like losing an arm or a leg.'

Sara was very depressed when she arrived home, although she did her best to put on a brave face for her father.

When Dominic suddenly arrived home with Marie, a Marie obviously in agony, both Sara and her father helped to get her to her room.

'Oh, God! Oh, God!' she kept groaning.

'What happened?' their father asked Dominic anxiously once they had got Marie into bed in her darkened room, leaving her as she seemed to drift off into a restless sleep.

Dominic paced up and down the lounge. 'Apparently the pain started in the night——'

'I thought so,' Sara sighed. 'She was very restless,' she explained. 'I—I went in and sat with her for a while.'

'She didn't tell anyone because she didn't want us to worry,' Dominic continued harshly. 'She finally half collapsed with the pain just after lunch.'

'This can't go on.' Sara's father shook his head. 'Just lately the headaches have become worse, more frequent, with much more pain. I—Oh, God, I'm afraid we're going to lose her!'

'No!' Sara denied shrilly. 'There's the operation.'

Dominic sighed heavily. 'Marie says no.'

'But we can't just let her die!'

He put a hand up to his temple. 'I've tried to talk her into having the operation, but she won't even listen to me.'

'Then maybe she'll listen to me,' Sara told him fiercely. 'I won't let her die without putting up a fight!'

'Marie isn't you, Sara,' Dominic said softly. 'You would fight, Marie would rather die than risk being paralysed or retarded.'

'That isn't true,' she denied harshly. 'Do you know how terrified she is of dying? Death petrifies her, gives her nightmares. In fact, I'm sure it's this fear that triggers off half of her headaches.'

'She told you about—about this fear?' her father rasped.

'Yes.'

'Then I want you to try and persuade her to have the operation. I think if anyone can do it you can.'

She hesitated. 'Dominic?'

He looked at her with tormented eyes. 'I agree with your father, you're the only person who might be able to do it.'

'Then I'll try.'

'Thank you.' He squeezed her hand.

She had to try and save her sister, even if it meant losing any chance of ever being able to have Dominic herself. There could never be any happiness for her with Dominic anyway; she could always only ever be Marie's substitute.

Marie was moving about restlessly when she entered the room, wide awake. 'Is the doctor coming?' she groaned.

'Yes.' Sara soothed her brow as she had the night she had stayed with her. 'And when he arrives I want you to agree to have this operation.'

'No!' Marie shuddered. 'Never! I don't want to be a vegetable in a wheelchair, unloved and unable to love.'

Sara held her tightly to her. 'You must know Dominic will always love you, no matter what happens.'

Marie looked up at her with wild frightened eyes. 'No man could love me if I were like that.'

'Dominic would,' Sara said with certainty.

'No. No, he wouldn't. He would hate me——'

'You know that isn't true. Marie, you're my sister, a part of myself,' she gripped her arms tightly. 'Wouldn't you rather die fighting?'

'I don't want to die at all!'

'I know that, darling, I know. But we all have to die some time. I know which way I would prefer.'

Marie shook her head. 'You're different from me.'

She knew that, Dominic had just told her so, and there was no question about which one of them he preferred. And if it were humanly possible she was going to bring Marie through this for him.

'I may be different from you, Marie,' she said with determination. 'But if I had someone in love with me, someone who wanted to marry me, to be with me for ever and ever, then I'd want to fight this thing.'

Marie's eyes were huge. 'You would?'

'Of course.' Sara's voice became less heated as she realised Marie was actually listening to her now. 'You can't just sit back and let life deal you a blow like this. You have to have this operation, for yourself, for Dad, and most of all for Dominic.'

'And for you too?'

'Yes, for me too.' Sara blinked back the tears, wishing she could stop being so emotional. She couldn't be helping the situation.

Marie was calming. 'You would stay with me all the time?'

'As much as they would let me,' Sara agreed eagerly.

Marie bit her lip. 'I'm not sure . . .'

'Just think of the future, Marie.'

'The future?' she sighed. 'There hasn't been one to think of lately.'

'Well, think of it now. Think of being with the man you love for all time, of having his children.'

'Oh yes,' Marie gave a dreamy smile, 'I would like that, Sara.'

'Then take the one chance you've got. Please!' she added pleadingly as Marie still seemed to hesitate. 'Children, Marie,' she repeated, although the thought of Marie being the mother of Dominic's children caused her actual physical pain. 'Children who look just like their father,' she said softly, achingly.

Marie drew a ragged breath. 'I—I'll do it,' she said after long troubled minutes.

Sara swallowed hard. 'You—you will?'

'Yes,' her sister nodded.

'You won't change your mind?'

Marie licked her dry lips. 'No.'

Sara hugged and kissed her, both of them laughing and crying at the same time, Marie's headache apparently forgotten.

A knock sounded on the door before Dominic entered the room. 'The doctor's here, Marie,' he frowned as they both beamed at him. 'What's happened?'

Sara stood up. 'I'll leave you two alone.' She moved to the door, unintentionally brushing past Dominic as she went out, her breath catching in her throat at the warm vitality of him. 'I—er—I'll send the doctor up in a minute.' She hastily closed the door and fled down the stairs.

When Dominic came down a few minutes later he was somewhat dazed. 'How did you do it?' he asked Sara softly.

She didn't even pretend to misunderstand him. 'I pointed out what a lovely future she had as your wife,' she looked down, biting her bottom lip, 'as the mother of your children.'

'And that caused this change of heart?'

Her head went back. 'Yes.'

'Well, of course it would,' her father said excitedly. 'We should have thought of it before, Dominic, should have talked about the future instead of the present. God, I don't care how it came about, I'm just glad she's agreed at last.' His arm went about Sara's shoulders. 'I don't know how to thank you.'

'I don't want or need thanks. I just hope that Mr Forrester can operate now, before Marie has time to have second thoughts.'

Dominic frowned. 'Do you think she might?'

She swallowed hard. 'Not if I keep reminding her of her future as your wife.'

'Sara——'

'I think I can hear Mr Forrester,' she interrupted

brightly, turning towards the door, swallowing down the raw emotion she felt at Dominic's husky exclamation. Why couldn't he leave her alone now? Couldn't he see how the thought of him and Marie as husband and wife was breaking her up.

Simon Forrester looked very pleased when he came into the room. 'If I could just use your telephone, Michael? I want to get Marie to hospital as soon as possible.'

'You're going to do it now?' Sara's father asked. 'Today?'

The doctor nodded. 'I don't think we have any time to lose.'

After that things moved very fast. The hospital room was arranged, the ambulance sent for. Sara herself went in the ambulance with her sister, Dominic and her father following behind in Dominic's car.

'She's already sedated,' the doctor warned Sara as she joined Marie in the ambulance. 'So don't expect a great deal of conversation from her,' he smiled, patting her hand comfortingly.

For the first part of the journey Marie seemed to be asleep, but Sara sat and held her hand anyway, sure that her sister could feel her presence beside her, could even draw on some of her strength to help her get through this.

It felt weird to be travelling through London in an ambulance, the siren wailing to warn the other traffic of the seriousness of the patient inside.

'Sara? Sara!' Marie opened bleary eyes; their journey was almost over.

'I'm here,' Sara reassured her, bending forward into Marie's vision.

'Tell him I love him, Sara. No matter what happens I want you to tell him I love him.'

'He already knows,' Sara said huskily

'No,' Marie shook her head, her voice slurred from the sedation. 'No, he doesn't know. Tell—tell Danny I love him.'

'Danny?' Sara repeated sharply, frowning heavily. 'Surely you mean Dominic? Marie, it's Dominic you love, Dominic you're going to marry.'

'Tell—tell Danny I love him,' Marie repeated, dozing back into a drugged sleep.

Sara frowned. Tell *Danny* she loved him?

CHAPTER TEN

IT was a long night, not least because of Sara's utter confusion about Marie's emotions. Had she really meant for her to tell Danny, Dominic's brother, that she loved him? It didn't seem very likely. Marie had probably been confused by the sedative, had gone back into the past, to last summer when she and Danny were dating. Consequently, Sara didn't make that call to Danny, sure that there had been some sort of mistake.

Dominic looked ghastly, pacing the waiting-room they had been shown into like a caged lion. There were lines of tension beside his mouth, a greyness beneath his tan, and the last thing he needed to be told right now was that Marie had talked of another man before falling asleep.

The operation seemed to have been going on for hours, and the strain of it all was beginning to tell on their father. He looked haggard, dark shadows beneath his eyes, a weary droop to his shoulders.

'How the hell much longer are they going to be?' Dominic muttered, but received no answer as he continued to talk to himself in that low angry tone.

Sara stood up. 'Would either of you like a cup of coffee?'

Her father gave a wry smile. 'I think it's starting to run out of my ears already.'

'Oh.' She sat down again.

'I'll have one,' Dominic requested huskily.

She stood up again. 'Black?'

'Please,' he nodded.

He didn't really want the coffee, he knew it and so did she, but Dominic had sensed her need to do something, to feel useful at a time when they were all powerless to do what they really wanted to do, and that was to save Marie.

She was out in the corridor, putting money into the coffee machine, when Danny walked into the hospital, a plaster across the bridge of his nose.

'How is she?' he immediately demanded to know. 'How's Marie?'

'We don't know yet,' Sara shrugged. 'She's still in theatre.'

He drew a ragged breath. 'I came as soon as I found out. Do you have any idea how long they'll be?'

'None,' she told him gently, aware that if her father and Dominic looked ill, Danny looked ten times worse.

'Where's Dominic?' he scowled.

'With my father.'

Danny sighed, gingerly touching his nose. 'Do you think he would mind if I waited with them?'

'I'm sure he wouldn't,' she assured him warmly. 'I doubt he even remembers your fight, Danny.'

'Probably not,' he acknowledged heavily.

'Come on!' She took hold of his arm.

Her father gave Danny an absentminded nod as he recognised him, while Dominic scowled heavily when he saw his brother, evidence that he hadn't forgotten their last meeting at all.

'Your coffee.' She left Danny to cross the room to Dominic, holding out the plastic cup to him.

'Thanks.' His expression was brooding as he took it. 'What's he doing here?' His eyes were narrowed on his brother.

She put her hand on his arm. 'He heard about Marie,' she explained softly. 'He's concerned, Dominic.'

'Yes,' he sighed. 'Yes, I suppose he is.'

'Go and talk to him,' she encouraged.

'Mm, I suppose I should apologise for breaking his nose.'

Her eyes widened. 'It really is broken?'

Dominic nodded. 'So my mother informed me. She

wasn't very happy about the situation. Danny and I used to argue when we were younger, but not lately.'

'It was my fault, I'm sorry,' Sara sighed. 'I should have explained what had happened, but I was just so shocked.'

'Of course you were.' He squeezed her hand. 'I just—I jumped to conclusions.'

'As you have about Eddie too,' she put in softly.

Dominic frowned, his eyes narrowed as he looked at her searchingly. 'Is that the truth?'

She met his gaze unflinchingly. 'Yes.'

'Thank you for that,' he again squeezed her hand. 'I'd better go and reassure Danny that I don't intend turning violent on him again. He looks as if he could do with some reassuring about something.'

'It's Marie. He—Danny——'

'I know,' Dominic cut in harshly. 'I'm well aware of my brother's feelings towards Marie. He loves her, he's always loved her.'

Sara's eyes widened. 'Knowing that you still asked Marie to marry you, even though you must have realised how hurt your brother would be?'

'Danny's feelings were considered——'

'And discarded,' she scorned, turning away. 'As mine were. Go and talk to Danny by all means, although whether or not he wants to speak to you is another matter entirely.'

'Sara——'

She shook off his hand. 'Just go, Dominic,' she told him vehemently.

'I'll go, for now. But we'll talk again, Sara. There are some things I have to tell you.'

Her head went back. 'There's nothing I want to hear from you. Please go and talk to Danny, I have to go to my father.' She walked away before he could make any further move to stop her.

Her father looked even worse now, and Sara made him sit down, holding his hand tightly as the door opened and Simon Forrester came in, still in his gown from operating.

The surgeon looked very tired. 'Surgically I've done everything I could,' he told them. 'Now we'll just have to wait and see.'

They took it in turns to sit with Marie through the night and most of the next day, and her father and Dominic were both with her when she woke up.

Sara had been sent home to rest, but she knew by her father's face when he arrived home that Marie had come through the operation with no harm to herself. She instantly started to cry, the strain of the last few days finally taking over.

'Hey!' her father chided, his relief obvious. 'You're supposed to be happy, not burst into tears!'

'I am happy,' she wailed. 'Is she really all right, Dad? Is it really all over?' She blinked back further tears.

'Really.' He crushed her to him. 'She asked for you.'

'Then I'll go to her. I——'

'Calm down, Sara!' he laughed, looking younger now that the tension was finally over. 'She's resting now, you can see her later.'

That first meeting with her sister was an emotional one, and during the next few weeks they became closer than ever, Sara spending most of her time at the hospital—when Dominic wasn't there. Dominic she avoided at all costs.

The bandage was finally removed from Marie's head, revealing that it would be a long time before the two of them were again confused with each other. Marie's hair was now a blonde downy thatch only half an inch long. But she was alive and out of danger, and that was the important thing.

'I feel ridiculous!' She put up a selfconscious hand to her hair.

Sara smiled. 'You look beautiful.'

'That's what Dominic said,' Marie told her ruefully.

Sara's smile became brittle. 'Well, he should know.'

Dominic was the one to drive Marie home when the time came for her discharge, his arm about her waist to support her into the house. At the first sight of him in several weeks all Sara's love towards him came bounding back, her lashes instantly lowering over her revealing eyes.

It was agony to watch his solicitous concern for Marie, so she made her escape as quickly as she could, using a visit to Eddie as her reason for excusing herself.

'Sounds serious,' Marie teased. 'Doesn't it, Dominic?'

'I don't know.' His gaze was intent on Sara. 'Is it?'

She daren't look at him, daren't risk giving herself away. 'I don't know that myself yet,' she said lightly; knowing that she was lying. Eddie and she were friends, and that was all they would ever be. 'I'll let you know if it is.'

'Before the wedding, I hope,' Dominic said tautly.

'We mustn't tease her,' Marie laughed.

Sara made good her escape, wondering how Marie had ever gained the impression that Dominic was teasing. He had been deadly serious, his expression grim.

When she arrived home later that evening Marie called her into her bedroom, patting the side of the bed for her to sit down beside her.

Sara did so. 'Shouldn't you be asleep?'

'Yes,' Marie grinned. 'But I wanted to talk to you. How's Eddie? I like Eddie.'

'He's well,' Sara replied guardedly.

Her sister laughed. 'I really was only teasing earlier about you and Eddie being serious.'

'I hope so,' she grimaced. 'Eddie is in no more of a hurry to get married than I am.'

'Dominic is.'

Sara looked up sharply. 'Dominic is what?'

Marie sighed. 'In a hurry to get married.'

Sara licked her suddenly dry lips. 'Is he?' she said brightly. 'Well, you've been engaged for some time, and now that you're well I suppose——'

'He doesn't want to marry me, Sara,' Marie interrupted.

'Don't be silly!' Sara's smile seemed to be fixed on her lips, a bright meaningless smile. 'Of course he wants to marry you——'

'No,' Marie insisted softly. 'And I don't want to marry him. You remember what I said to you the night of my operation?'

'A-about loving Danny?' It hadn't been mentioned since!

'Yes,' she nodded. 'Well, I do. I always have.'

Sara gasped. 'But—but Dominic!' This didn't seem to be making sense at all.

Marie sighed. 'It's a little complicated.'

'A little?' Sara scorned. 'I can't make any sense of it!'

'You will, I'll explain it to you. You see, Danny and I argued last summer, I can't even remember why now. Anyway, Dominic took me out for a while to try and cheer me up. Then I fell down the stairs,' she sighed. 'Danny came rushing round to see how I was, but—well, even then I think I must have sensed there was more wrong with me than they first realised, and I turned Danny away. But he kept coming back, and then when I found out about my injury I knew I had to stop him.'

She swallowed hard. 'With Dominic?'

Marie nodded. 'But it was with Dominic's consent. We never intended getting married, I just couldn't agree to marry Danny knowing I was going to die. So Dominic and I became engaged, and Danny finally left me alone. You do see, don't you, Sara? Danny would be hurt less that way?'

'Maybe. But I think he should have been given the choice.'

'No,' Marie shook her head. 'He would only have been noble, insisted on marrying me anyway.'

Sara frowned, trying her best to understand. 'Where did Dominic stand in all this?'

Marie smiled. 'Dominic is the best friend I ever had.'

'Friend? But you haven't been behaving as if you were just *friends*.'

'All acting,' her sister grinned. 'Enjoyable acting, I'll admit, but acting just the same. Then tonight he started discussing weddings for real.' She frowned. 'I couldn't understand it.'

'He loves you——'

'No, he doesn't,' Marie laughed at the thought of it.

'But——'

'He really doesn't love me, Sara, he just thought *I* wanted to marry *him*.'

'He did?'

'Yes, and that was your fault. Yes, it was,' Marie insisted as Sara went to protest. 'You told Dominic it was the thought of being his wife and having his children that had encouraged me to face the operation. What you said to me was that I had to think of being with the man I loved for ever and ever. And I did that—I thought of Danny.'

'*Danny?*' Sara gasped.

'Yes,' her sister smiled happily. 'I'm going to marry Danny. And you love Dominic, don't you?'

'I——'

'Don't you?' Marie quirked an eyebrow.

Sara licked her lips. 'Yes.'

Marie nodded. 'I told him you did.'

'You did *what*?'

'Don't look so annoyed,' Marie smiled. 'He didn't believe me.'

'Thank God for that! Don't you realise——'

'He loves you too, Sara.'

She paled. 'He—he what?'

'He loves you,' Marie repeated happily. 'I had my suspicions, the way you kept avoiding each other and everything, but tonight I knew for sure.'

'H—how did you know?'

'He told me,' Marie announced calmly.

Sara was beginning to wonder if she were hallucinating. Marie had only got engaged to Dominic so that Danny wouldn't get hurt, the man she really loved, and Dominic had aided her in this plan. And now Marie was going to marry Danny after all, and Dominic had admitted to Marie that he loved her, Sara. None of it sounded very plausible, and yet Marie seemed very confident.

'See?' Marie held up her bare left hand. 'No engagement ring. Danny is going to buy me one tomorrow.'

'Oh, he does know about this, then?' Sara mocked dazedly.

'Silly!' her sister giggled. 'Of course he knows about it, although he was furious with Dominic and I when he found out what I had done.'

'I'm surprised he understood it!'

Marie eyed her teasingly. 'Don't you want to know more about Dominic loving you?'

Sara blushed and stood up to turn away. 'I don't believe he does. Oh, I know he's attracted to me, but only because I look like you. I think you're wrong about him not loving you, Marie. He must be very upset about your marrying his brother.'

'Not at all. He went and got Danny himself once I'd explained the misunderstanding to him.'

She shrugged. 'Just a cover up to his real feelings——'

'What does it take to convince you?' Marie said impatiently. 'The man loves you, he wants to marry you.'

'M—Marry me?'

'That got your attention, hmm?' her sister teased. 'Of course Dominic wants to marry you, but he says you don't want him.'

'But he knows I do—I mean—well——' Sara blushed scarlet. 'I do,' she said lamely.

Marie's eyes twinkled mischievously. 'I won't ask how he knows. The thing is he doesn't,' she sobered. 'He says you despise him.'

She had only said that in the heat of the moment, surely he realised that. But it seemed not. She was almost afraid to believe what Marie was telling her, and yet her sister seemed so confident.

'I've never seen him like this before,' Marie continued at her silence. 'Dominic's always been like an older brother to me, always confident and in command—that's why I turned to him for help. But he's as uncertain as a schoolboy about you. I'm not sure I like to see him like that.'

'So you intend putting him out of his misery?' Sara was beginning to hope, to believe what Marie was telling her. Could Dominic have really meant it that night he had told her he loved her? Oh, God, she hoped so!

'No, I want you to do that. Tonight.'

'Now?' she exclaimed.

'Why not?' Marie shrugged.

'Because it's after twelve o'clock at night!'

Marie grinned. 'I'll make your excuses to Daddy in the morning.'

'In the——! Even if I did go and see Dominic now I'd be back tonight,' Sara claimed indignantly.

'Of course you would.'

'I would!'

'I just agreed, didn't I?' Marie gave her a look of exaggerated innocence.

'It was the way you agreed.'

Marie smiled. 'I know Dominic.'

'Do you indeed?' Sara's eyes flashed jealously.

'Not like that,' her sister laughed. 'There was never anything like that between us. Now with you it's different, he goes all tense and white about the mouth when he talks about you—so much so that once he gets you alone I know he won't let you out of his sight.'

'Okay,' Sara sighed, 'you convinced me. I'll go and see him.'

'Take my car.' Marie searched through her handbag for her keys. 'Daddy was going to buy you a car, but now that you're getting married I suppose Dominic will buy you one.' She held out the keys with a mischievous smile.

'Don't jump ahead,' Sara warned. 'No one said I was getting married.'

'You will be. Poor Daddy will be totally confused!'

Sara only wished she felt as confident about Dominic's feelings as Marie seemed to be. Could it really be true, had Dominic just been pretending with Marie, could it really be that she was the one he loved? Only he could tell her that.

He answered the door to her himself. 'Marie called me,' he revealed deeply.

Sara gave an angry sigh. 'I know she's my sister, and I love her dearly, but she's an interfering busybody.'

'She just called to tell me to expect you, Sara, nothing else.'

'Oh.' She bit her lip nervously. 'Can I come in?'

'Of course.' He opened the door wide. 'Although if you do,' he added huskily, 'I doubt I'll be able to let you out again.'

So Marie was right, she had to be. Sara looked up at Dominic with steady brown eyes. 'I don't want you to,' she said softly. 'I don't ever want to leave you again.'

Dominic swallowed hard, seeming to sway where he stood. 'God, I love you!' he groaned achingly.

She fell into his arms, holding him so tightly her arms ached. 'I love you, too,' she choked, any last doubts dispelled.

He pressed featherlight kisses down her throat, his lips warm and fevered. 'Marie told you everything?'

'Everything,' she nodded, raising her mouth invitingly. 'I'm so sorry I ever doubted you.'

'It was my fault for not telling you the truth. I wanted to—God, how I wanted to, but I couldn't break a confidence like that, not even for the woman I love. And you are the woman I love, Sara.' His mouth lowered to hers.

He was like a thirsty man in a desert, devouring her with his love and passion, his caresses heated, and he carried her over to the sofa. They lay close together, murmuring words of love between caresses, hours passing as if minutes, lost to each other as they frantically tried to convince each other of their love.

Dominic lay against her breasts, his arms possessive. 'The first time I saw you I knew you were the most beautiful thing I'd ever seen.'

'You thought I was Marie!'

He shook his head. 'I don't think I did, not even then. I was excited just looking at you, and that had never happened with Marie.'

'She assures me you're only friends,' Sara taunted, smoothing the darkness of his hair.

'We are. Marie has always been like a kid sister to me, you were something else completely, right from the first. I become aroused just looking at you.'

'Dominic!' she blushed her confusion.

'But I do. I want to love you, darling.' He kissed her bare breast.

'Yes.'

'You said that once before, in exactly the same way——'

'And you turned me down,' she remembered with pain.

'Because of your innocence! I was tied to Marie, by loyalty if nothing else, and it wasn't fair to involve you when I couldn't marry you.' He caressed the soft curve of her breast with his tongue.

'Did you want to marry me even then?'

'I did, and I do. Will you marry me, Sara?'

'Yes! Yes to marriage, and yes to——'

He put silencing fingers over her lips. 'I can wait until after we're married.'

'Well, I can't.' She looked at him with love-drugged eyes. 'I want to stay with you tonight, Dominic. Tonight and every other night.'

He gave a rueful smile. 'Tonight I might get away

with, then I think we'll have to wait until after the wedding. Otherwise your father might take a shotgun to me.'

Sara held him fiercely to her. 'I'm so glad I came to England, so glad I found my father and Marie, and so very, very glad I found you. I love you so, Dominic.'

'And I love you too.' He picked her up and took her into the bedroom, to the first night of a lifetime of nights together.

AN AGE-OLD GAME WITH WORDS

In Harlequin novels, North American readers frequently encounter words and phrases that are unquestionably British—and occasionally unfamiliar. Sometimes it's easy to determine the meanings of these expressions from the context, but there is one type of English speech that, unless you're in the know, is virtually impossible to understand—cockney rhyming slang, an amusing game with language that many Londoners have played for centuries.

In this slang, words are replaced with phrases that rhyme with the words. Here are a few common examples:

boots	daisy roots
deaf	Mutt and Jeff
eyes	mince pies
face	boat race
head	loaf of bread
mate	China plate
mouth	north and south
stairs	apples and pears
suit	whistle and flute
wife	trouble and strife

Just to further puzzle the unsuspecting listener, the cockney tends to drop the latter part of the slang phrase, so that, for instance, a suit is called a whistle, and boots are called daisies. If ever you hear an Englishman use an expression that completely baffles you, perhaps now you'll be able to "use your loaf" and work out the meaning for yourself!

Legacy of
PASSION
BY CATHERINE KAY

A love story begun long ago comes full circle...

Venice, 1819: Contessa Allegra di Rienzi, young, innocent, unhappily married. She gave her love to Lord Byron—scandalous, irresistible English poet. Their brief, tempestuous affair left her with a shattered heart, a few poignant mementos—and a daughter he never knew about.

Boston, today: Allegra Brent, modern, independent, restless. She learned the secret of her great-great-great-grandmother and journeyed to Venice to find the di Rienzi heirs. There she met the handsome, cynical, blood-stirring Conte Renaldo di Rienzi, and like her ancestor before her, recklessly, hopelessly lost her heart.

Readers rave about Harlequin romance fiction...

"I absolutely adore Harlequin romances! They are fun and relaxing to read, and each book provides a wonderful escape."
—N.E.,* Pacific Palisades, California

"Harlequin is the best in romantic reading."
—K.G., Philadelphia, Pennsylvania

"Harlequin romances give me a whole new outlook on life."
—S.P., Mecosta, Michigan

"My praise for the warmth and adventure your books bring into my life."
—D.F., Hicksville, New York

*Names available on request.

Take 4 these best-selling novels FREE

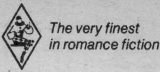